The Night House Files

CLASSIFIED

Praise for *The Deadsoul Project* ...

"The perfect balance of thrills and chills ... It's a little bit *The X-Files*, a little bit Stephen King-lite and a lot of frightening fun" ***THE TIMES* CHILDREN'S BOOK OF THE WEEK**

"Reads like a classic sci-fi horror and was full of moments that made the hairs on the back of my neck stand up – especially the ending!" **CYNTHIA MURPHY**

"*The Deadsoul Project* is a relentlessly gripping thriller ... ingenious, brilliant and terrifying" **JONATHAN STROUD**

"It built to a climax so tense that I held my breath for what seemed like longer than humanly possible" **JENNIFER KILLICK**

"This chilling read has elements of *The X-Files*, *Doctor Who* and more. Historical fiction with a terrifying difference!" **LESLEY PARR**

"A chilling horror/sci-fi rollercoaster ... *The X-Files* meets *Alien* ... I think I may have held my breath for the entire duration" **PHIL HICKES**

"Mystery, conspiracies, gore and horror make for a tense and compulsive story ... not for the faint of heart" ***IRISH EXAMINER***

"A similar vibe to *Stranger Things* ... a thrilling read that pits kids against alien bodysnatchers" ***INIS MAGAZINE***

Praise for *The Wintermoor Lights* ...

"Perfect for horror fans ... Innovative, sophisticated and creepy as hell" **CHECK 'EM OUT BOOKS, BLOG**

"80s nostalgia pulses through this eerie story ... Luke Brookes's fantastic illustrations match this vibe and ramp up the fear" **SCOPE FOR IMAGINATION, BLOG**

"An incredibly gripping read ... Another unmissable and compelling case from The Night House Files" **BOOK CRAIC, BLOG**

"Guaranteed to set hearts racing and send shivers down their spines" **MRS SYDNEY'S FAMOUS WORLD'S SMALLEST LIBRARY, BLOG**

THE NIGHT HOUSE FILES

THE HOUSE OF HORRORS

Dan Smith

Illustrated by

Luke Brookes

Barrington Stoke

Published by Barrington Stoke
An imprint of HarperCollins*Publishers*
1 Robroyston Gate, Glasgow, G33 1JN

www.barringtonstoke.co.uk

HarperCollins*Publishers*
Macken House, 39/40 Mayor Street Upper,
Dublin 1, DO1 C9W8, Ireland

First published in 2026

ISBN 978-0-00-879090-5

10 9 8 7 6 5 4 3 2 1

A catalogue record for this book is available from the British Library

Printed and bound by CPI Group (UK) Ltd, Croydon, CR0 4YY

FSC
www.fsc.org
MIX
Paper | Supporting
responsible forestry
FSC® C013604

For the weird and the wonderful!

The Night House Files

Officially, the Night House does not exist. But it is real. It is an old and secret organisation that investigates the truth behind strange events around the world; events that include the paranormal, the extra-terrestrial and the bizarre. Events that governments do not want you to know about. The findings of these investigations are filed and kept safe by a mysterious person known only as the Nightwatchman. Once a year, the Nightwatchman delivers a file to me. My job is to turn the contents of the file into a story so that you can know the truth. That is the Nightwatchman's wish, and I dare not disobey.

The following story is taken from File FL1779: The House of Horrors.

Everything you are about to read is true. The names of people and places have been altered to protect the innocent.

Excerpt from article on mond0bizarro.com dated March 2022

mond0bizarro.com

Mond0 BIZARRO

March 2022

What really happened at Coyote Creek?

Hey, truth-seekers, how about this for a weird little story? Between 2017 and 2019, thirty-two people were reported missing in a large area of the Chihuahuan desert in West Texas. For a long time, the police were completely clueless. It was as if the people just disappeared off the face of the earth. Abducted by aliens, you might think. Or perhaps it was a new “Bermuda Triangle”. Well, we still don’t really know. But what we *do* know is that in July 2019, events led police to an abandoned town two miles from the lonely desert highway.

The town was called Coyote Creek.

It was a so-called "ghost town", which aren't unusual in West Texas. Abandoned mining towns and other failed communities litter the harsh desert landscape. But Coyote Creek was hiding a dark secret. You see, in the middle of the town, among the broken and collapsing buildings, police discovered a large house. Inside that house, they found the "remains" of all those missing people. All thirty-two of them. The exact state of those "remains" has never been made public, but rumours tell of strange cults, outlandish waxworks and even the undead.

For a short time in July 2019, Coyote Creek was a hive of activity. Police and federal investigators were on site for several days, and witnesses report seeing many vehicles entering and leaving the area.

But soon after the investigation was over,

almost all records were lost in a fire. Everything went up in smoke like someone was trying to get rid of evidence. The house itself was demolished, along with the rest of Coyote Creek, and now there is no trace of the town or of what happened there.

The whole incident smells like a cover-up to us at mond0bizarro.com. There's an "official" version of events, but we just don't believe it. Something bizarre happened in that house – something that would make your hair stand on end. Government experiments maybe? A Satanic cult? Alien invaders? No one really knows for sure – except the people who were there and those who covered it up.

So, fellow conspirators, what do you think *really* happened in that old house in Coyote Creek? And why are the authorities covering it up? Put your thoughts in the comments.

West Texas Desert

Tuesday, 23rd July 2019

What you are about to read is an account of the terrible misfortune that happened to the Slade family: a British family who were on the trip of a lifetime to the United States of America. After spending two days in San Francisco, the family intended to drive across the country to visit Mrs Slade's sister, who lived and worked in Dallas, Texas. The family plotted their route carefully, planning to visit several places of interest along the way. But even the best-made plans can fail. And sometimes things go horribly wrong.

We join the family several days into their trip,

inside a rental car, driving through the night along a dark and lonely desert highway. The air was warm, but a strong wind had been gathering since sunset. Grit and sand swirled across the faded tarmac road, sparkling in the car's headlights. Above, stars filled the clear sky, but not a single other light was visible. Not even the tiny pinpricks of a distant town on the horizon. The world was utter darkness.

In the back of the car, leaning his head against the window, fifteen-year-old Jay Slade was drifting in and out of sleep. Every now and then he caught snippets of his mum and dad whisper-arguing in the front.

"Are you sure we're not lost?" Mrs Slade was saying. "It feels like we're lost. We haven't seen a building for miles. Not even another car." There was an edge of worry in her voice.

"Of course we're not lost," Mr Slade reassured her. "The highway is literally a straight line through the desert. Not even *I* can get lost on a straight road," he laughed. "Anyway, we saw a car just a few miles back."

"That was twenty minutes ago," Mrs Slade told him, then she sighed heavily. "We should never have taken that detour to Roswell. Stupid UFO museum."

"It wasn't stupid," Mr Slade argued. "It was interesting. And Jay loved it."

It was true. Jay *had* loved it. His mum had spent the whole time rolling her eyes, looking bored, but Jay thought it was cool. Sure, the aliens and the flying saucer looked about as fake as you could get, but all the information was fascinating. And while Jay didn't quite believe that there had really been a UFO crash at Roswell, he liked the idea of it. He *wanted* to believe.

He was still wearing the cap his mum and dad had bought him from the gift shop. It was all black, with a green alien face on the front. The words THEY'RE HERE were stitched on the back, also in green.

"Well, we shouldn't have spent so long in there,"

Mrs Slade went on. "Now we're going to be late to Anika's."

"We won't be late for your sister's birthday," Mr Slade said. "That's why we're driving through the night. Another five hours and we'll be there – just as they're getting out of bed. So we'll make it on time. OK?"

"If we have enough petrol," Mrs Slade grumbled.

"Gas?" Mr Slade replied in an awful American accent. "We've got plenty o' gas, little darlin'. Don't you be frettin' about nothin'."

"And it's creepy out here." Mrs Slade ignored her husband's attempt to be funny. "All that darkness. No one around. I don't like it."

"You think there might be aliens out there?" Mr Slade continued with his shocking American accent. "Well, don't you worry about nothin'. You're safe with me, little lady. I'll tell you what, why don't we put on some good ole music and—"

BANG!

The car jerked violently, throwing Jay forwards. His seatbelt dug into his chest, and his head slammed against the seat in front of him. He bounced back into his own seat with such ferocity that pain fired through his neck and shoulder. The air was filled with a nerve-shredding scream of metal tearing across the surface of the road.

"What the hell?" Mr Slade exclaimed as he slammed on the brakes.

Jay lost all sense of direction as the small car skidded out of control. Sand billowed all around them, reflecting the bright yellow headlights in a dazzling display that flickered around the inside of the vehicle. It was light then dark as the car spun through the cloud, shuddering dramatically.

The scream of metal on tarmac grew louder as Mr Slade fought to bring the vehicle under control, and then, finally, the car stalled and juddered to a stop.

There was a long moment of stunned silence.

The Slade family sat cocooned in the car, surrounded by dust clouds as they tried to figure out what had just happened.

"Oh my God," Mr Slade whispered eventually. "Is everyone OK?" He checked his wife, asking, "Tiya? Are you hurt?"

"No." She shook her head once, then they both turned to look in the back seat.

"Jay?"

Jay was wide awake now, shocked and bruised from the bump.

"Um ... I'm fine," Jay stuttered. "I think." He took off his cap and rolled his head from side to side, wincing at the pain.

"What the flip just happened?" Elisha asked.

Jay looked at his older sister sitting beside him in the back seat. Her black hair fell forwards over her brow, half-covering her dark eyes. There was a concerned expression on her face.

"Did we hit something?" she wondered.

Jay stared at Elisha for a long moment. His thoughts were fuzzy, and he had a weird feeling he couldn't quite explain. Of course he was shocked by what had just happened, but … he had a deep sense that something else was wrong. Something other than the car crash.

"I don't know," Mr Slade said, taking off his glasses and rubbing his face. "Maybe. Or maybe a flat tyre. Is everyone sure they're OK? No one's hurt?" He glanced at his wife, who was massaging her neck and frowning at Elisha.

"We should get off the road," Elisha said. "In case another car comes, right? I mean, look."

The wind had cleared the dust now, blowing it away into the night, and Jay could see that they had come to a halt at an angle across the centre of the highway. The headlights were still on, shining out into the desert.

"We should move, right, Dad?" Elisha said, looking directly at Mr Slade.

"Yeah," said Mr Slade, shaking his head to clear it. He pinched the bridge of his nose, then put his glasses back on. "You're right. We should get off the road."

Jay's stomach was churning, and his thoughts were spinning. He couldn't think straight. He told himself it was because of the accident – the adrenaline, the shock, the pain – but there was something else that was nagging at him, buried under all of that.

As he tried to figure it out, his dad turned back to the wheel and started the ignition. The engine sparked into life, and the car lurched before stalling again.

"Sorry," Mr Slade muttered before starting the engine again and slowly moving the car forwards. Immediately, there was a horrible squeal of metal. A piercing sound that drove through Jay like fingernails on a chalkboard. The whole car juddered and shook.

"Feels like a flat tyre," Mr Slade said, gripping

the wheel to control the vehicle as he guided it, rattling and shaking, to the side of the road. "I'll have to check." He sat for a moment, then took a deep breath. "Everyone stay in the car."

He popped open his door, slipped out and quickly slammed it behind him to stop the dust from blowing in.

The wind buffeted the vehicle, rocking the suspension as Jay watched his dad head round to the front of the car. Out there in the gathering storm, Mr Slade squinted against the bright headlights and swirling sand as he half raised a hand to them, then he crouched down, dropping out of sight.

When he stood up again, he was frowning.

"What is it?" Mrs Slade said to no one in particular.

Mr Slade glanced behind him, into the darkness. He stood like that for a few long moments, his head cocked to one side as if listening, then gave up and made his way around the right-hand side of the car.

Jay turned to watch him and found himself, once again, looking at his sister, Elisha, sitting beside him.

Elisha was facing forwards, staring through the windscreen.

"You've got sand on you," Jay said, almost without thinking.

"What's that, bro?" Elisha turned to look at him.

"You've got sand on you. In your hair."

"Have I?" Elisha raised a hand to her head. "Oh, yeah. Thanks." She rubbed her hair to brush it away, but Jay noticed there was more sand on the shoulders of her leather jacket. And on her jeans.

"How?" Jay asked. "How have you got sand on you?"

Elisha shrugged. "It must have come in through the door when Dad opened it just now. Look – it's all over the seat."

Jay blinked hard and glanced at the seat between him and his sister. She was right – it was covered with a dusting of sand.

"Oh yeah," Jay said. "Weird. I didn't notice."

"Not surprised." Elisha smiled and put a hand on Jay's shoulder. "I think we're all a bit shaken up."

"Yeah," Jay agreed.

At that moment, Mr Slade yanked open the driver's-side door. The sudden blast of wind took Jay by surprise, making him jump. The storm blew into the car as Mr Slade climbed back into his seat. He slammed the door shut, re-sealing them all inside.

"Well?" Mrs Slade asked.

Mr Slade paused, then took off his glasses and blew the dust off them. "It's the weirdest thing."

"What is?" Jay asked.

"Well ... it's all of them," Mr Slade said, staring out into the storm. "All four tyres. They're all flat."

"*All of them?*" Mrs Slade repeated. "They're *all* flat? But ... how is that even possible?"

REPORT: X5J02011-1

CLASSIFIED

TOP SECRET

Interview with Jay Slade

Date: Wednesday, 31st August 2022

After the tragedy that happened to his family at Coyote Creek in 2019, Jay Slade was brought back to England, where he was placed in the custody of Dr Hooper at the Katja Psychiatric Institute. He was non-verbal for six weeks. When he finally spoke and told his version of events, Jay was diagnosed with "severe delusional disorder". He remained in the secure psychiatric hospital until August 2022 when, aged eighteen, Jay was released into the custody of his grandparents.

A Night House agent was able to speak with Jay in August 2022 by pretending to be a journalist investigating the incident at Coyote Creek.

NIGHT HOUSE AGENT: You're sure all four tyres were damaged?

JAY SLADE: Yes. Of course I'm sure.

(The Night House agent notes that Jay Slade's attitude was generally hostile during the interview, consistent with someone who is both frustrated and angry. It is the agent's view that Jay was accustomed to people not believing his version of events.)

JAY SLADE: And by the way, I don't care what the doctors or the police say. It was *all four tyres.* Every single one. They're trying to make out like I imagined it or something, but I didn't. I'm telling you, I—

NIGHT HOUSE AGENT: It's OK, Jay. I'm not the

police, and I'm not a doctor. I'm here to listen to you – to get to the truth.

JAY SLADE: You don't want the truth. You want me to—

NIGHT HOUSE AGENT: Jay. I *do* want the truth. Just tell me everything as you remember it.

JAY SLADE: Fine. Well, the *truth* is that all four tyres were flat. And when Dad told us, I was like, "What the hell?" I mean, it didn't make sense. Who has four flat tyres at the same time? No one, that's who.

NIGHT HOUSE AGENT: So how do you think it happened?

JAY SLADE: How should I know? Elisha said maybe it was like a cattle grid or something. You know, like we went over it and it burst our tyres. Or a pothole.

NIGHT HOUSE AGENT: Do you think that's possible? You said it was very windy that night. There was a lot of sand and dust in the air. Visibility would have been low. Perhaps your father, Mr Slade, didn't see a—

JAY SLADE: You don't get four flat tyres from a cattle grid. Jeez, they don't even *have* cattle grids across roads like that. What do you think I am? Stupid?

NIGHT HOUSE AGENT: No. I don't think—

JAY SLADE: It was something else. Had to be.

NIGHT HOUSE AGENT: Like what?

JAY SLADE: You see – you don't believe me. I don't have to talk to you.

(At this point in the interview, Jay stood up as if he wanted to leave. It took some time to persuade him to continue.)

NIGHT HOUSE AGENT: Jay, it's important that you understand I do *not* disbelieve you. I'm on your side. But I want to build a picture of what happened. To find out the truth.

JAY SLADE: OK, well, the truth is that those freaks did it. I don't know how, but they did.

NIGHT HOUSE AGENT: You mean the people from Coyote Creek?

JAY SLADE: I mean the *freaks* from Coyote Creek.

NIGHT HOUSE AGENT: OK, we'll come to that later. For now, let's concentrate on what happened next. After your father saw that all the tyres were flat.

JAY SLADE: After that? I guess we checked our phones for service, but there wasn't any. Not even a single bar. It was like a dead spot or something. So we were in the middle of nowhere, it was dark, it was windy and we couldn't call for help.

NIGHT HOUSE AGENT: And then you saw lights?

JAY SLADE: Yeah. Bright lights behind us. And they were coming fast. Like, *crazy* fast.

West Texas Desert

Tuesday, 23rd July 2019

Everyone turned to look back through the rear window. Bright lights burned through the billowing sand into the interior of the car. And whatever those lights belonged to, it was racing towards them at high speed.

"It's going to ram straight into us!" Mrs Slade gasped.

A moment later, Jay heard the roar of an engine welling up beneath the rush of the wind. He gripped the back of the seat and squinted against the lights that grew brighter as the engine grew louder. It was a deep and edgy growl that soon totally drowned out the sound of the storm. It thundered towards them like an unstoppable express train.

"Oh my God," Elisha muttered. "What the hell is it? It's going to kill us."

But then its brakes slammed on, and it came to a sudden stop *right* behind them.

There couldn't have been more than a few centimetres between their bumpers.

Whatever it was, it was big – much bigger than their rental car – with bright lights that poured into the car like a supernova.

Jay lowered his head so the peak of his cap blocked some of the light, and he held up a hand to shield his eyes. Like that, he could just about make out the rounded bonnet of a vehicle and the shape of a grille. Above that was a narrow, dirty windscreen, with a dark figure looming behind the wheel.

"Is that a truck?" Mrs Slade whispered.

For a few long seconds, the vehicle just sat there, aggressively revving its engine again and again.

"What are they doing?" Mrs Slade stared back through the gap between the front seats. "I don't like this." Her face was pale in the cold light. The dark circles under her eyes shone grey like mould on an orange.

Jay felt a loose and watery sensation in the pit of his stomach. They were miles from anywhere. He had seen enough films about people lost on lonely highways to understand that this was a dangerous situation for them.

Then the truck honked its horn.

It wasn't a high-pitched "beep" like cars on the roads at home in England. It was a loud and deep rumble. Like a foghorn sounding across a stormy sea. It echoed around the inside of the car and lingered in their ears.

"What does he want?" Jay whispered, glancing at Elisha, who was also looking through the back window. "Why is he beeping?"

"What do we do?" Mrs Slade asked.

"We stay calm," said Mr Slade. His voice was quiet, and the words seemed almost stuck in his throat. "Everything is going to be fine."

Jay's heart thumped harder when the driver's-side door of the truck swung open and a large figure emerged into the night. The person stepped forwards and stood still for a second, silhouetted by the headlights, then headed towards the Slades' car.

Mr Slade said something, but his words came out as a hoarse whisper. He cleared his throat and nodded. "It's fine. Everything is fine."

But Jay wasn't so sure.

As the person came closer and passed the rear window of the car, Jay could see that he was a tall and sinewy man, hunched against the storm. He was wearing a light blue buttoned shirt with dark blue patches across the chest, then jeans and boots. He had thick dark eyebrows and a bushy grey moustache. The wind blew his long grey hair around his head like he was some kind of demon appearing from the storm. He glanced into the back of the car as he passed. His piercing eyes stared right at Jay, then across at Elisha beside him.

The stranger came to the driver's side of the Slades' car, then he lifted a hand and tapped his large calloused knuckles on the window.

Mr Slade pressed a button and let the window slide down a quarter of the way.

The man put his hands either side of the window and glared into the car. "What the hell are you doing out here?" he growled. His voice was deep and laced with a Texan accent. "You can't just stop in the middle of the road."

"I'm sorry," Mr Slade said. "We've had—"

"I almost ran into the back of you, goddammit."

"—an accident," Mr Slade finished.

The man paused. "An accident, you say?"

"Ye-yes," Mr Slade said. "That's right."

The man's face changed in an instant. The anger fell away and was replaced with a warm smile.

"Well, why didn't you just say so? Hell, I'm sorry if I scared you folks. You're not from around here, right?"

"Err, no," Mr Slade said. "We're from the UK."

"Brits?" the man asked. "Well, how about that? You'd better get ready for some proper Texan hospitality. Pleased to meet you. My name is Sam."

He reached a large hand in through the quarter-open window and held it out for Mr Slade to shake.

Mr Slade lowered the window further and shook Sam's hand. "I'm Mike. This is my wife, Tiya, my son, Jay, and my daughter ... Elisha."

Still holding Mr Slade's hand, Sam leaned in to get a good look at everyone. His gaze lingered on Elisha, and he gave her a quick nod that, for some reason, filled Jay with a terrible sense of dread.

"Nice cap," Sam said to Jay. "You been up to the museum at Roswell, I guess?"

"Err. Yeah," Jay replied.

"And now you got into an accident and lost all four tyres, eh?" Sam said, taking back his hand. "That's unlucky. You folks musta hit a mighty big pothole."

Jay thought it was odd that Sam knew all four tyres had burst. He was certain his dad hadn't mentioned it to him. The only explanation was that Sam had seen the burst tyres when he walked over to the car. In the dark. In the middle of a dust storm. Before Jay could question him though, Mr Slade asked, "Is there a garage close by?"

"A garage?" Sam repeated, but he pronounced it "gu-raaj". He sucked his teeth and shook his head. "Nu-uh. Not close. I'd say the nearest is forty miles back the way you just came."

"Oh no," Mrs Slade complained. "Now we'll never get to my sister's on time."

Sam gave her a questioning look.

"My wife's sister," Mr Slade explained. "She

lives in Dallas. It's her birthday tomorrow – or *today*, actually – and we promised we'd be there."

"Oh my, that's a tough one," Sam agreed.

"I don't suppose you have a working phone, do you?" Mr Slade asked. "The rental came with breakdown cover. I'd call from mine, but we're not getting any signal."

"There's no signal for miles round here. Some kind of dead spot." Sam looked both ways along the highway, squinting against the wind and the dust, then took a deep breath. "Lucky for you, I can help you out. I have spare tyres at my place. It's close by. There should be some that'll fit your car."

Mr Slade looked at his wife, then back at Sam. "That's very kind. So ... if we wait here, you could—"

"I won't leave you out here," Sam said. "I've got a winch on my truck. I'll pull you up on the back and take you with me. Fix you up and have you on your way in no time."

From where he was sitting in the back seat,

Jay saw his mum put her hand on his dad's arm.

"We don't want to be any trouble," she said. "Maybe you could just take us to the nearest garage?"

Sam smiled and smoothed his moustache with his finger and thumb. "That's fifty miles away. In the dark. It's well out of my way even before you take this storm into consideration."

"Forty," Jay said.

"Hmm?" Sam turned to him quickly, something dark flashing in his eyes. "What did you say, boy?"

"You said *forty* miles to the nearest garage before," Jay reminded him. "Not fifty."

Sam kept his eyes fixed on Jay. "Forty, fifty, what's the difference? Everything's a long way from here – except my place." He turned to smile at Mrs Slade. "Safest thing is to go to mine, fix you up, wait for the storm to pass, send you on your way. Get you to your sister on her birthday. Nothing's more important than family, ain't that right?" He looked at Jay and winked. "I can even offer you a coffee and a slice of the best damn pecan pie in all of Texas."

Mrs Slade shared a look with Mr Slade, then glanced back at Jay.

"I can tell you folks are unsure, and I don't blame you," Sam said. "You don't know me. I could be a psy-cho-*path* for all you know. Just itching to get out my chainsaw." Sam chuckled at his own joke. "Or I could be a Good Samaritan who just wants to help. Tell you what – why don't you talk it over? I'll give you a minute or two, but then I'm gone. I have family too – Mom and Pop waiting at home. They ain't well, and I need to get back to them. Don't take too long."

Sam tapped the top edge of Mr Slade's open window with the palm of his hand, then turned and headed back to his truck.

West Texas Desert
Tuesday, 23rd July 2019

"This feels wrong," Mrs Slade said as soon as Sam was gone. "We don't know him. We can't just let him tow us away somewhere. It feels wrong."

"Mm." Mr Slade nodded as he put the window up. "You're right."

"What choice do we have?" Elisha butted in. "What else are we going to do? Just sit here? I say we're lucky he came along."

Their voices were like distant echoes to Jay. He felt strange. Almost as if he wasn't there, separated from his own body. He stared absently at the back of the seat in front of him, trying to remember the conversation they'd had with Sam: something about whether it was forty or fifty miles to the nearest garage. And about the tyres.

"All four," Jay said to himself.

"What did you say?" Elisha asked.

Slowly, Jay turned towards his sister, who was leaning back in the seat, half in shadow. She was staring at him through strands of dark hair that fell across her eyes.

"What did you say?" she asked again.

For a moment, Jay looked right through Elisha, unable to focus. His thoughts slithered around his mind like oily mist.

"Bro?" Elisha prompted him.

Jay closed his eyes and shook his head, bringing himself back to the world.

"All four tyres," he said. "That's weird, isn't it? I mean, what if it was deliberate? What if that guy had something to do with it?"

"You mean Sam?" Elisha replied. "No, I don't think so. He seemed nice."

"He doesn't know how close the nearest garage is," Jay reminded her. "First he said forty miles, then he said fifty."

"Everyone makes mistakes," Elisha told him. "I say we're lucky he came along, otherwise we could be out here all night. Even longer. I haven't seen any other cars, have you?"

"No." Jay shook his head, but he still didn't feel *lucky* that Sam had come along. He felt *afraid*.

"I think we should trust him," Elisha said with a smile. "What do you say, Dad?"

Mr Slade looked at Elisha as if he was trying to work out the answer to an extremely complicated question.

"Dad?" Elisha prompted him. "We should trust him, right?"

Mr Slade smiled. "Yes, of course, darling. Of course we should trust him."

"Mum?" Elisha asked.

Mrs Slade nodded slowly. "Yes. We should trust him."

"Wait. What?" Jay said. "We don't even—"

"It's going to be fine," Elisha interrupted. "You'll see."

Jay looked through the back window at the truck on the road behind them. He squinted against the headlights that burned like fiery suns. Jay couldn't see Sam sitting behind the wheel, but he could sense him. And he didn't like it. There was a cold feeling in his stomach, and his blood pulsed in his head. *Thump. Thump. Thump.*

Something was wrong. But it would be many terrifying hours before he learned exactly what it was.

REPORT: X5J0209-1

CLASSIFIED

TOP SECRET

Excerpt from: FBI Report

Date: 25th July 2019

Secretly obtained by Night House agents

County police were first on the scene at the house in Coyote Creek but contacted the FBI* soon after.

In the course of their investigations, FBI agents searched a customised Chevrolet '41 truck parked at the front of the house. It was one of several vehicles found by county police close to the house at Coyote Creek on 23rd July 2019. The customised truck was in poor condition, dented in places and with much of the original blue paint chipped away to reveal rust in the metalwork.

The vehicle was fitted with a winch that had been used to pull a second, smaller vehicle onto the flatbed. The second vehicle was identified as a Kia Rio, which had been rented at Los Angeles International Airport under the name Mr Michael Slade. All four tyres on the Kia Rio were punctured.

In the cab of the Chevrolet '41, county police found a loaded shotgun and two custom-made devices that were handed over to the FBI. The first device was an extendable, spiked metal belt, similar to a "stinger" used by police officers to stop vehicles. When thrown across the road, the hollow metal spikes pierce a vehicle's tyres, deflating them instantly.

***FBI - Federal Bureau of Investigation. The principal federal law enforcement agency of the United States.**

West Texas Desert
Tuesday, 23rd July 2019

When Sam's truck rolled past and pulled up in front of the Slades' rental car, Jay saw what a beast it was. Rusted and battered, it looked as if it had been through a hurricane and only just survived.

Sam jumped down from the cab and came over to speak to Mr Slade, who had lowered his window just far enough to hear what the stranger was saying.

"You ready to go?" Sam shouted over the howl of the growing storm. His long grey hair whipped around his face.

"Sure," Mr Slade replied. "Thank you."

"You made the right decision," Sam said. "Just sit tight and I'll hook you up – get us out of here before you know it. This truck may look old, but she's strong." He winked at Jay, then headed back to his vehicle.

Jay watched him drop two narrow ramps from the back of his truck, then climb up onto the flatbed to grab the huge hook that hung from a winch. Hunched and battling the wind, Sam carried the hook down, dragging with it the steel cable that wound around the drum of the winch. He bent down and attached the hook somewhere under the front of the Slades' car.

"Well, I suppose it's an adventure," Elisha said.

"Mm," Jay's dad agreed. "Very kind of him to help."

Jay watched his dad and told himself that everything was OK. If his mum and dad were fine with this, then it must be safe. But he couldn't shake the apprehension that gnawed at him. His hands felt clammy, and something was making the back of his head tingle.

The car lurched, and Jay turned his attention to the front of the car once more. Sam had started the winch. There was tension as it began to turn, pulling the steel cable tight, then it started to drag their small car onto the back of the truck. Mr Slade gripped the steering wheel to keep the tyres on the narrow ramps, and Jay felt himself pushed back against the seat as if they were driving uphill. The winch's motor whined over the sound of the wind.

Finally, the car levelled out, the high-pitched whine stopped and there was a release of tension as the winch stopped turning.

When the car was secure, Sam withdrew the ramps, gave them a thumbs up, then jumped back into his truck and set off.

Jay sat silently in the back of the car as Sam carried them deep into the stormy night. There was no turning back now.

—

Before long, they turned off the highway onto a smaller road. The rental car shook and creaked on the back of the truck as they jostled along the rudimentary track. The wind howled around them.

"We must be almost there," Mr Slade said when they eventually saw the first silhouettes of buildings appear in the swirling dust and sand.

But as they passed among them, they saw only dilapidated and crumbling shapes. Small wooden buildings with collapsed roofs and broken windows. A tumbledown gas station with rusted pumps and crumbling stone walls lost to the desert. The skeletons of sand-blasted vehicles lay among them like tombstones.

"What is this place?" Jay wondered aloud.

"Some kind of ghost town," his mum said. "I heard there were places like this. Old mining towns, that kind of thing."

"It's creepy," Jay whispered.

"Don't be so pathetic," Elisha teased him. "It's cool."

"Doesn't feel like it," Jay replied. "Feels scary."

"Look." Elisha pointed at a collection of faint lights ahead, and soon a large building appeared out of the darkness. Several of the windows had the dim glow of lights behind heavy curtains or blinds.

Sam guided his truck towards the house, taking the family closer and closer.

"We're here," Elisha whispered as Sam brought the truck to a stop.

At that exact moment, bright security lights flicked on, and for the first time, the Slade family saw the house that was to become their tomb.

Still in the car, perched on the back of the old truck, the Slade family peered through the dirty windscreen and surveyed the house. The red-brick building looked out of place in the desert. As if it had been transported there from the centre of a city in another country. Built on two storeys, it loomed over the family, eager to swallow them up. Wide front steps tumbled forwards like a diseased tongue from the shadow of a covered porch.
On both sides of the enormous front door, tall windows glowed dimly, winking in the storm like wicked eyes.

The ground in front of the building was littered with old broken wood and sheets of dented corrugated steel that rattled and hummed in the wind. Tufts of straggly grass bowed to the storm.

Mrs Slade took a hair bobble from around

her wrist and tied her curly brown hair back into a ponytail. She leaned close to the windscreen. "I don't see any tyres," she whispered.

"Or a garage," Jay added.

"Must be round the back," Elisha suggested. "It's fine, Mum. Right, Dad?"

"Yeah," Mr Slade agreed, his voice robotic and calm. "Everything's fine."

Sam climbed out from the cab and came to the side of the truck. He motioned for Mr Slade to roll down the window.

"Let's get you inside," Sam shouted. "Out of the storm."

"Come on," Elisha said, popping the door on her side.

So they obeyed. They opened their car doors and jumped down from the back of the truck where their car creaked and rattled in the wind.

They put on their jackets, then followed

Sam towards the building and climbed the front stairs like unthinking sheep being corralled into a slaughterhouse.

When they reached the top of the stairs, Jay noticed something painted on the wall beside the huge front door. It was some kind of lettering, nearly as tall as he was, but it had been blasted to almost nothing by the desert climate. Jay had to step back to figure out what it said:

DR KILGORE'S HOUSE OF HORRORS

"Coyote Creek used to be an oil town," Sam explained when he saw Jay reading the sign. "The oil dried up, and everyone left except Mom and Pop. Pop had a love of making things out of wax and thought maybe he could build an attraction that would give this place new life."

Sam smoothed his moustache with his left hand. "People come from all over to see Roswell or the Marfa lights. They look for aliens, Chupacabra or La Lechuza. So why not a House of Horrors? A museum for all the secrets of the desert. Well …" Sam reached down and gripped the door handle in his fist. "Maybe Pop will tell you about it."

He turned the handle and pushed the door open.

Elisha was the first to step inside. Mr and Mrs Slade followed, but Jay hesitated on the threshold. As if he knew that entering the house would be a final act – the point of no return.

"Come on," Elisha encouraged him with a grin. "What you waiting for?"

Without intending to, Jay stepped forwards.

As he did so, he looked up at Sam, who was holding the door for him. For a second, it was as if a cloud had moved away from Jay's thoughts, and he saw something that terrified him.

The friendly look on Sam's face had dropped away, replaced by a hungry grin that chilled Jay's

HOUSE
OF
HORRORS.

bones. Like Sam was a fox circling a henhouse. Then Sam reached out, took the cap off Jay's head and placed it on his own. He adjusted the peak so it was pointing directly forwards, and he winked one eye.

"All right with you, sport?" he said in a quiet voice.

Jay suddenly wanted to run. He wanted to call out to his family and warn them not to enter the building.

But it was too late. Sam's hand was on Jay's back, pushing him inside. And as soon as Jay was in, Sam stepped back out into the night and pulled the door shut, leaving Jay and his family trapped inside Dr Kilgore's House of Horrors.

The dim hallway echoed with the sound of Sam clicking locks into place from outside.

REPORT: X5J0209-2

CLASSIFIED

TOP SECRET

Interview with: Jay Slade

Date: Wednesday, 31st August 2022

After the tragedy that happened to his family at Coyote Creek in 2019, Jay Slade was brought back to England, where he was placed in the custody of Dr Hooper at the Katja Psychiatric Institute. He was non-verbal for six weeks. When he finally spoke and told his version of events, Jay was diagnosed with “severe delusional disorder”. He remained in the secure psychiatric hospital until August 2022 when, aged eighteen, Jay was released into the custody of his grandparents.

A Night House agent was able to speak with Jay in August 2022 by pretending to be a journalist investigating the incident at Coyote Creek.

JAY SLADE: Being inside that house was like being inside a museum. It had that feel to it, you know? That *smell*. All old and musty. We were in a kind of hallway with dirty tiles on the floor, patterned like a chessboard. Black and white. Some of them were cracked and broken. There was, like, wood panelling on the walls, and there was a disgusting red carpet running from the front door all the way up the wide stairs to the floor above.

NIGHT HOUSE AGENT: You could see all that? I thought you said it was dark in there?

JAY SLADE: I'm not lying.

NIGHT HOUSE AGENT: Of course.

JAY SLADE: Yeah, it was dark, but not *dark* dark. There was *some* light. It was coming from a chandelier over the middle of the hallway, but it was dirty, like everything else, and a lot of the bulbs didn't work, so the light was bad. But I could see where we were. I could see the wooden banister running around the … the, what do you call it? The landing upstairs. That was chipped and broken too. And there were posters in frames, you know? To advertise what was in the museum. The exhibits.

NIGHT HOUSE AGENT: Do you remember any of them?

JAY SLADE: Yeah, there was something about witch trials, I think. And one that said "Survive the Torture Dungeon". I remember that because I saw it later. The torture dungeon, I mean. We went in there. That's where …

(Jay was silent for a while at this point, and the Night House agent had to encourage him to continue.)

NIGHT HOUSE AGENT: Do you remember anything else about what you saw when you first went in?

JAY SLADE: There were waxworks at the bottom of the staircase leading up to the first floor. One on each side, but I'm not sure what they were supposed to be. They were sort of twisted up, like they were people who were transforming into something else. Like half animal, half human. I think maybe they were supposed to be Skinwalkers or something. And then this big pink neon sign flicked on.

NIGHT HOUSE AGENT: A neon sign?

JAY SLADE: Yeah. It said "DR KILGORE'S HOUSE OF HORRORS", and it was pink, which is weird, right? Well … everything about that place was weird. But it was like it was trying to be welcoming even though it totally wasn't. It was freaking terrifying.

NIGHT HOUSE AGENT: What did you do?

JAY SLADE: Nothing. We just kind of stood there for a bit. Stunned. Like, it was so creepy and … and then everyone snapped out of it. Dad grabbed the front door handle, trying to get out, but it didn't open. He pushed and pulled on it, but it was locked. Mum was getting all panicky, and she banged on the door, calling out "Hello!" Stupid, right? I mean, who's going to answer? Sam? I don't think so – he was the one who locked us in. It was obvious we were in deep shizzle. So we all did what people do – we got out our phones. But there was nothing. No service. No GPS. No nothing. We were on our own, and I started to feel like those freaky waxworks were watching us. Like they were alive. I even thought I could hear them breathing, you know? In and out. In and out. And fear started to swallow me up like I was falling down a long, cold tunnel.

REPORT: X5J0209-2

CLASSIFIED

TOP SECRET

Excerpt from: FBI Report

Date: 25th July 2019

Secretly obtained by Night House agents

The second device found in the Chevrolet '41 truck that was parked in front of the house in Coyote Creek was an unidentified electronic device, approximately 7 x 4 x 2 inches, with multiple antennae at the top. The device was not immediately identifiable and has been taken to Abilene for expert identification.

REPORT: X5J02017-1

CLASSIFIED

TOP SECRET

Interview with: Simon Teller

Date: Monday, 5th September 2022

In 2019, at the time of the Coyote Creek incident, Simon Teller was working as a technician at Everything Electronic in Abilene, Texas. An agent from the Night House visited Simon Teller at his home to conduct the interview.

Simon Teller was described as being 62 years old, six feet tall, white, male, overweight. He had dark hair, greying at the sides, and a heavy beard. His home was cluttered with cardboard boxes, old newspapers and electronics.

NIGHT HOUSE AGENT: Can you confirm that, in July 2019, an electronic device was brought to you by the FBI?

SIMON TELLER: Ha ha! Oh my, yes, I can. It's hard to forget a thing like that. It was the most exciting thing that ever happened to me in that place.

NIGHT HOUSE AGENT: And do you know of any reason why the FBI didn't take the device to an in-house team?

SIMON TELLER: Seemed like they wanted a quick answer, and they didn't have anyone as good as we were. Not close by, anyhow.

NIGHT HOUSE AGENT: I see. Can you describe the device for me, please?

SIMON TELLER: Well, if I ain't losing my marbles, I remember it being pretty unremarkable. A black plastic box about the size of a small radio – the kind you might have in your kitchen. There were four or five antennae on the top. No obvious branding or markings.

NIGHT HOUSE AGENT: Did you know what it was?

SIMON TELLER: My guess is that it was some kind of jammer. To block phone signals and GPS and whatnot. You can buy these things easy now, and probably even easier in a few years' time, but three years ago? It was pretty unusual to see something like that.

NIGHT HOUSE AGENT: So it would stop a mobile phone – a cell phone – from working?

SIMON TELLER: If I'm right about what it was, then yes. It would stop a cell phone from sending or receiving signals. And I mean any kind of signal.

NIGHT HOUSE AGENT: You sound unsure that it was a jammer.

SIMON TELLER: I wouldn't say "unsure". More like, I knew what it was but didn't get the chance to test it properly. See, it was very peculiar because the agent who brought it to me came back just a couple of hours later and took it away again. He seemed agitated.

NIGHT HOUSE AGENT: As if he'd made a mistake bringing it to you?

SIMON TELLER: You can say *that* again. He told me to forget I'd ever even seen it. Said that they'd know if I talked to anyone. It felt very much like a threat.

NIGHT HOUSE AGENT: Really? But you're talking to me. You're not afraid?

SIMON TELLER: No way. I'd tell anyone who asks. Maybe some who didn't. It feels good to stick it to the "man".

Coyote Creek, West Texas Desert
Tuesday, 23rd July 2019

"We have to get out of here," Mrs Slade said, slipping her phone into the hip pocket of her cargos. "I don't even know why we agreed to ... whatever we agreed to." The heels of her boots tap-tapped on the hard tiles as she left Mr Slade and Jay still trying their phones and headed towards a large wooden door on the right-hand side of the hallway.

"I feel strange," Mr Slade said, taking off his glasses and pressing his fingers into his eyes. "Why *did* we come here?"

"There must be a way out," said Mrs Slade.

Dirty white paint peeled in long strips from the door, and a crooked sign hung above it, displaying the words "Old West Cannibals". To one side of it stood the waxwork of a tall man shrouded in a dark fur coat with bushy grey tails draped over each shoulder. His hat was the snarling head of a wolf, its mouth open just enough to display its savage teeth. The wolf's beady black glass eyes stared dead ahead.

Mrs Slade rattled the door handle.

"Locked," she said through gritted teeth and went to the next door. "Locked," she said again.

"What about this one?" Jay said, heading for the first door on the left. It was guarded by the figure of something that looked more or less like a werewolf. It was human shaped, muscular and had crude, coarse hairs protruding from its waxy face. Yellow eyes seemed to watch Jay as if the creature might come to life and pounce at any moment. The wonky sign above this door read: "Desert Horrors".

Jay tried not to look at the werewolf-thing

as he reached out for the door handle. He expected it to be locked like the others, but to his surprise the handle turned. The latch clicked, and the door creaked open, just enough for Jay to see that it was dark on the other side.

He stopped and looked back at his family, silently wondering what to do next. There was a moment of stillness in the hallway, then the others came to join him. They moved slowly and deliberately, as if too much noise could harm them.

"I think we should go in," Elisha said.

"What if there's something in there?" Jay replied, wincing when his words echoed around the hallway. He lowered his voice and went on. "What if there's something bad?" Now he couldn't stop himself from glancing up at the mangy werewolf standing guard. It smelled like wet dog, and it was giving him the creeps.

"Or what if there's a way out?" Elisha suggested, more hopefully.

Jay looked at his dad, who swallowed and

nodded before stepping in front of Jay and pushing the door open wider.

"Hello?" he said as he leaned in. "Is anyone there?"

"Shh," Mrs Slade told him. "Be quiet."

It was pitch-black beyond the door. The only light was that which slithered in from the hallway. Jay had the impression he was peering into a cave.

"There must be a window," Mrs Slade said, which reminded Jay he had seen lights in the windows when they first arrived. "Or another door."

"Which would be a way out," Elisha said. "So one of us should go in and check it out. Don't you think, Dad?"

"Wait a minute." Jay pulled his phone from his pocket. He switched on the torch and directed the white light into the room. It didn't penetrate far into the thick and oily darkness, but it allowed them to see into a corridor leading away from the door.

Faded paint on the walls of the corridor depicted an image of the desert, with rugged mountains in the distance beneath a pale blue sky. Spiky cacti and balls of dry tumbleweed filled the foreground. The floor was covered with a layer of dirt which might have been brought in from the desert outside. Further along the corridor, there was a wide gap in the wall on the right-hand side, cordoned off with a thick rope at waist height.

Jay lifted his torch higher and saw there was something behind the rope. Some kind of alcove or small room, maybe, and there were silhouettes of figures.

"It's a display room," Mr Slade said. "For waxworks. Maybe this is all part of the experience. You know, to make us scared or … or …" His voice trailed away as if he knew he wasn't doing a very good job of convincing anyone that this was normal. There was something very wrong about this whole situation, and they all knew it.

"Well, someone has to go in," Elisha said. "To see if there's a way out. The rest of us should wait here by the door."

Jay looked at his sister.

"In case the door closes," Elisha explained. "And locks us in."

Mr Slade took a deep breath and nodded. "You're right. I'll go. You all stay here." He took his phone from his pocket and was about to switch on his torch when Jay stopped him.

"Save the battery," Jay said. "We might need it. And I'm coming with you."

His dad didn't argue, and Jay knew he was glad to have company as they left Elisha and his mum waiting by the door.

Jay's trainers crunched on the gritty sand as he followed his dad along the path. His own heavy breathing echoed around him. The walls seemed to press inwards, suffocating, and the corridor disappeared into darkness beyond the reach of his phone torch. Jay had that feeling again – that he was an animal being corralled along a corridor in a slaughterhouse; that there was nothing ahead other than certain death.

No way out.

But as they came closer to the roped-off area, the silent darkness was shattered by a piercing howl. Jay jumped so suddenly that his phone fell from his hand with a clatter. A moment later, there came a series of long, blood-curdling screams, together with snarling sounds. Bright lights exploded above them.

Jay's heart faltered. Fear and shock fired through him like a jolt of electricity. His eyes closed and he flinched, putting his hands up to his face. Then his heart re-started at double-time, hammering in his chest, pumping icy blood through his veins.

As the sounds of struggling continued, Jay heard his dad swear loudly.

When Jay opened his eyes, his dad was right beside him, staring across the rope cordon.

On the other side of the rope, illuminated by spotlights hanging from the ceiling, was a small area displaying the set-up of a campsite. Badly painted background boards showed a faded desert scene that continued around the walls from the corridor. The ground was decorated with rock and sand as if it were part of a shallow canyon. In the centre was a campfire made from fake logs. Cloth flames flickered upwards, moved by some kind of blower from beneath the logs.

Beside the fire was a crude canvas tent surrounded by pots and pans and other old-fashioned camping items. In the foreground, close to the rope cordon, a waxwork figure lay on the ground with his shirt unbuttoned and his chest torn open. Ripped flesh and broken ribs glistened in the bright spotlights.

Beside him, another wax figure – a young woman – was on her knees, recoiling in horror from the beast that stood over them. The creature was not unlike the thing that was guarding the door outside. Huge and terrifying, its flaking skin was smothered with tufts of mangy hair. Its muscular form towered over the woman as it reached its twisted claws towards her. Its lips were peeled back

in a permanent snarl, and strings of gore stretched between its vicious teeth.

As Jay stared in awe at the impossible beast, the looping sounds of screaming and snarling quietened, and a man's deep voice echoed through the room.

"Skinwalkers are witches from Navajo culture that can change their form," the voice explained. "They possess speed, strength, mimicry and mind-control."

There was a *click* as the sound cut out, then the room was left in silence once again.

Jay could hear his own heart thumping in his ears as he stared at the scene in front of him. But he wasn't looking at the slaughtered man or the beast that stood over him. He was looking at the kneeling woman. In particular, he noticed the way her bare feet protruded from the folds of her skirt. There was a tattoo on the bone of her ankle. Of a magpie. And despite everything that was happening, Jay couldn't help thinking that it was a bizarre detail to put on a waxwork.

News article taken from the MIDLAND TRIBUNE, dated 26th November 2018

Local Woman Missing

County police have been searching for a missing local woman, Felicity Thompson, aged 27. Miss Thompson had been visiting with her parents in Midland, Texas, for Thanksgiving and left to return home to Dallas on the morning of 24th November. She has not been seen or heard from since. Miss Thompson's parents, Mr Jim Thompson and Mrs Barbara Thompson, said that she left Midland in good spirits and intended to return directly to Dallas, where she lives with her boyfriend. Police ask that anyone with any information of Miss Thompson's whereabouts come forward immediately. Miss Thompson is described as 5 foot 6 inches tall, with dark hair and brown eyes. Distinguishing features include a mole below her right eye and a magpie tattoo on her left ankle.

Coyote Creek, West Texas Desert

Tuesday, 23rd July 2019

"Holy *flip*!" Mr Slade gasped as he put his hand on his chest. "I nearly peed myself."

Jay puffed out his cheeks and nodded. "Me too."

The realisation that the sudden noise and light wasn't going to harm them gave Jay a brief moment of relief, but then he remembered their predicament. They still needed to find an escape from the House of Horrors.

"We should keep going," Jay said, looking back

at his mum and Elisha standing by the slightly open door.

"Everything all right?" Jay's mum called.

"Yeah," Jay answered, picking up his phone. "Just got a shock."

"Hurry up!" Elisha gestured at them to go deeper into the room. "Find a way out."

"OK," Jay's dad nodded. "We—"

The lights above the tableau clicked off, and the room plunged into darkness. The suddenness of it was horrible – from bright to black in an instant – and Jay's eyes widened, hungry for sight.

"Torch, Jay." His dad's voice was flat and quiet.

"Oh. Yeah. Sorry." Jay switched on his phone torch and pointed it forwards.

"OK. Good," his dad said. "Let's keep going."

As they passed the display, Jay's phone threw light along the corridor, and the beast with the gore-flecked mouth cast a grisly shadow on the backdrop. The shadow thinned, elongated and then was gone as Jay and his dad continued onwards. When they came to a sharp corner, they peered around, Jay pointing the phone torch.

"How far do you think it goes?" Jay whispered. "Do you think there's an exit at the end?"

"No idea," his dad replied. "But there's only one way to find out."

Jay glanced back at Elisha and his mum. "Maybe we should—"

"Come on," his dad said, setting off again. "Let's get this over and done with."

Jay hesitated, then followed his dad, turning the corner and creeping further along the path. When he risked a look back, there was nothing to see but darkness. For all he knew, Elisha and his mum had been erased from existence.

"There's something there," Jay's dad said quietly.

Jay's heart raced as he whipped his head around to look. He squinted into the gloom expecting to see some shadowy monster blocking their path. A vicious alien with acid for blood or a maniac with an axe held high.

But it was none of those things. It was another gap in the wall, this time on the left.

"Could be another display," his dad said. "Or a way out."

Please let it be a way out, Jay repeated in his head. *Please let it be a way out.*

As they reached it, though, they were startled by a high-pitched screech, and spotlights clicked on over a second waxwork display.

This time, the wooden backdrop gave Jay the impression that he was looking into a farm. The back wall of the set was painted to resemble a large red barn, with a herd of dirty pigs in a pen on one side and a wonky chicken coop on the other. The coop was inhabited by what must have once been hens, painted in brown and white, but they were now too badly faded to look like anything other than messy blobs.

The centrepiece of the display was a waxwork man wearing dungarees and a grey shirt. He was standing beside a rusty plough and positioned to look as if he were stepping backwards with his hands raised to his face, covering his eyes. Dark blood ran between his fingers.

In front of him, on top of a pile of tatty hay bales, was a bizarre creature with the plump, grey-feathered body of a human-sized owl. Wide wings spread from its back as if it were about to take flight, and it had dangerously large talons that hooked like sickles into the hay bales. The talons, and the feathers around them, were covered in blood.

It was an awful thing to look at, but what made

it worse was that it was threadbare and dilapidated, like an ancient stuffed fox in a forgotten corner of an antique shop. Its feathers were falling out, and Jay could smell the decay and the dust from where he stood. But most horrifying of all was that the creature had a woman's head on its shoulders, turning it into a nightmarish fusion of human and owl.

Long, straggly hair that looked alarmingly real hung on either side of the woman's face.

"La Lechuza is a vengeful witch from Mexican and Texan folklore," boomed a deep voice. "She waits outside your window and whistles to attract your attention. But don't open the window and look out ... or she will have your eyes!"

As the voice was speaking, Jay was watching the third waxwork on the set – a tall, hooded figure that stood behind the human-owl creature. This figure wore jeans and a plaid shirt, as if it might be another farmer, but the hood over its head gave it a more sinister appearance.

The hood looked to be made from an old sack that was tightened at the neck with a piece of frayed rope. There were eye holes and a mouth hole cut into the sack, turning it into a crude balaclava. The figure was holding a wicked-looking axe in his right hand. But Jay was particularly interested in the figure's eyes because he was sure he had seen them blink.

As the voiceover continued with more details about La Lechuza, Jay stared at the hooded figure's eyes.

And he stared.

And he stared.

And ...

Blink.

There! It definitely blinked.

As Jay opened his mouth to say something to

his dad, the figure let out a blood-curdling howl and rushed forwards across the set. Mr Slade flinched away, and Jay stepped back in shock as the figure reached them. It grabbed Mr Slade with its left hand and grinned at Jay, baring its teeth through the mouth hole cut into the sack. Jay would have recognised that grin anywhere.

Then the hooded figure violently dragged Mr Slade backwards along the corridor. At that exact moment, the lights flicked off, and the room plunged into darkness once more.

Jay turned and ran.

X5JO2011-3

CLASSIFIED

TOP SECRET

Interview with: Jay Slade

Date: Wednesday, 31st August 2022

After the tragedy that happened to his family at Coyote Creek in 2019, Jay Slade was brought back to England, where he was placed in the custody of Dr Hooper at the Katja Psychiatric Institute. He was non-verbal for six weeks. When he finally spoke and told his version of events, Jay was diagnosed with "severe delusional disorder". He remained in the secure psychiatric hospital until August 2022 when, aged eighteen, Jay was released into the custody of his grandparents.

A Night House agent was able to speak with Jay in August 2022 by pretending to be a journalist investigating the incident at Coyote Creek.

NIGHT HOUSE AGENT: It must have been terrifying.

JAY SLADE: It was. I couldn't even think. I mean … I just ran. Without doing anything to help Dad. *Nothing.* I didn't try to stop it, to go after him or … anything. I just ran away. Like a coward. Like a scared little kid.

NIGHT HOUSE AGENT: But you *were* a scared kid, Jay. There was nothing you could have done.

JAY SLADE: Wasn't there? I should have *tried*. I should have done *something*. Then maybe Dad would still be here. If I had actually done *something*.

(At this point in the interview, Jay became silent and withdrawn. It was several minutes before he spoke again. When he did, his voice was quiet.)

JAY SLADE: I dream about it. About what happened to Dad. Mum too.

NIGHT HOUSE AGENT: Are you all right to continue, Jay?

JAY SLADE: Yeah.

NIGHT HOUSE AGENT: We can stop if you want to.

JAY SLADE: No. I want to tell you what happened.

NIGHT HOUSE AGENT: OK. So, you said the hooded figure looked at you?

JAY SLADE: Yeah. He looked at me. And I knew it was him. Sam.

NIGHT HOUSE AGENT: The man who helped

you on the road and then took you to the house? You're sure about that?

JAY SLADE: Yeah. And he wanted me to know it was him. To make me scared. Because that's what *they* wanted.

X5J0205-1

CLASSIFIED

TOP SECRET

Excerpt from: County Police Report

Date: 25th July 2019

Secretly obtained by Night House agents

Every window in the house at Coyote Creek – on both the first and second floors – was boarded up and painted over black. No natural light was able to penetrate the building. Electric lights were installed behind curtains in some of the windows to give the appearance of there being lights on in the house at night. Speakers were present in every room, all connected to a central sound system. The first responding officers to the scene were unable to enter many of the rooms, which were locked. In several of the accessible rooms, they found what at first appeared to be waxwork displays, all connected to lighting and sound systems. Officers noted that there was something strange about the waxworks themselves. **Closer inspection revealed them to be human, and some of them were still alive.*** The building was immediately sealed off as a major crime scene.

*Redacted from the original report.

REPORT: X5J02027-1

CLASSIFIED

TOP SECRET

Telephone interview with: Jerome Fitch

Date: Tuesday, 11th October 2022

In 2019, at the time of the Coyote Creek incident, Jerome Fitch was an officer in the local county police. It took Night House agents many weeks to locate a contact number for Jerome Fitch. He was reluctant to discuss the incident.

NIGHT HOUSE AGENT: You were one of the first officers on the scene at Coyote Creek. Is that correct?

JEROME FITCH: That's correct.

NIGHT HOUSE AGENT: Can you tell us about what you found? Specifically about the waxworks you saw at the scene.

JEROME FITCH: They weren't waxworks.

NIGHT HOUSE AGENT: What do you mean?

JEROME FITCH: I mean they were real.

NIGHT HOUSE AGENT: Can you explain what you mean?

JEROME FITCH: I don't know how else to say it. They were real people. We could've closed three years' worth of missing-persons cases if the FBI had let us. That's more than thirty families who could've found out the truth about their loved ones.

NIGHT HOUSE AGENT: So you're saying that the waxworks were actually real people?

JEROME FITCH: Exactly. And that Slade kid? After what I saw, and after the way the FBI shut us down, I believe everything he said. Every word of it.

NIGHT HOUSE AGENT: Were they still alive, the people you found?

JEROME FITCH: Alive? I'm not sure I'd say "alive" exactly.

NIGHT HOUSE AGENT: Can you tell me what you mean by—

JEROME FITCH: I … look, I'm sorry. I can't talk about this any more. I've already said enough.

(Jerome Fitch ended the call at this point and has refused any further contact with Night House agents.)

Coyote Creek, West Texas Desert

Tuesday, 23rd July 2019

When the hooded figure dragged Mr Slade into the darkness, blind terror took control of Jay. It was the kind of fear that burns with such intensity that there is no space in the mind for anything else. A fear that suffocates all thought and controls the body. When Jay ran away, he didn't even know he was doing it. He had no conscious control over himself as he stumbled through the darkness, back the way he had come.

The glare from his phone torch flickered and flashed along the corridor, which now felt miles long. The few seconds it took Jay to reach the corner felt like an eternity, and when he slipped on the dirt and crashed into the wall, he didn't pause even for a moment. The fear of some unspeakable thing following him, of it reaching out to snatch him away, was too much to bear.

Jay pushed himself off the wall and sprinted towards the open doorway where his mum and sister were waiting.

"Jay!" his mum gasped. "What happened?"

Jay couldn't speak. All he could do was barrel into his mum's arms and push her out into the corridor.

"Where's Dad?" his mum asked, tightening her arms around him. "What happened?"

"Dad?" Elisha called out. "Dad?!"

But there was no reply. There was nothing in the corridor but darkness and silence.

"He took him," Jay whispered, finally daring to turn and look back through the door. "He took him."

"Who took him?" his mum asked, holding

him tight. She was clearly trying to keep her voice calm, but the panic was difficult to hide. "What *happened*, Jay?"

Jay raised his phone to shine the torch along the corridor.

"Sam," he said. "The guy who towed us here. He had a hood on, like a sack, and, and—"

And he had an axe, Jay wanted to say, but he stopped himself. Should he tell his mum about the axe?

"And what, Jay?" his mum wanted to know.

"He took Dad," was all Jay could reply.

"So what do we do?" Elisha's voice cracked as she spoke. "*What do we do?*" She peered through the door into the corridor, then looked back out into the hallway.

Mrs Slade held Jay tighter. "We have to go after him," she whispered, even though she was starting to back away, desperate to protect her children. "We have to find him."

"How?" Elisha stammered. "Where did he go?

We can't see anything. What if Sam is still in there? You heard what Jay—"

"WELCOME!" A deep, gravelly voice boomed around the hallway.

Jay's heart lurched. He felt his mum's breath catch in her chest, and her arms tightened around him. Elisha stopped mid-sentence and moved closer to Jay.

"Welcome to Dr Kilgore's House of Horrors," said the voice.

It seemed to be coming from everywhere, echoing along the corridor in front of them and filling the hallway behind them.

"The hairs stand up on the nape of your neck," the voice went on. "Your palms are sweaty; your skin is cold and clammy. Terror folds around you. Your flesh creeps, and your heart thunders. You're wondering what to do. You're wondering where to go. But already you know it is hopeless. Once you enter the House of Horrors, you never, ever leave."

There followed a long, evil laugh that

reverberated around the building, then a click and everything went quiet. But Jay could still hear the laugh echoing in his ears. Like a dirty stain that refused to wash away.

"Who are you?" Mrs Slade screamed into the void of silence left when the voice stopped. "What do you want? Why are you doing this?"

There was no reply.

"Oh my God," Elisha whispered. "What the flip is going on?"

Jay could sense his sister's agitation. Elisha had been calm earlier, but now the panic seemed to be pulsing from her in waves. The pitch of her voice was rising, and her words were breathless. Jay felt it infecting him like an ugly contagion.

"We have to get out of here," Elisha gasped. "We have to escape."

Jay thought about what the voice had just said.

Once you enter the House of Horrors, you never, ever leave.

"But how?" Jay said, finding his voice. "How do we get out?"

"Where are the windows?" Mrs Slade said, looking back at the front door. "Why can't we see any windows? When we came in, there—"

"Wait!" Elisha cut her off. "What's that? Can you hear that?"

Jay and Mrs Slade stopped and held their breath to listen.

Shhhh. Shhhh. Shhhh.

It was the sound of shuffling footsteps scraping through gritty dirt.

"It's coming from down there," Elisha said, turning to look along the dark corridor beyond the door. The corridor Jay had just escaped from.

The shuffling grew louder, and Jay knew that whatever was making that sound, it was finding its way through the dark towards them.

"It's coming to get you!" a sinister voice whispered over the speakers. "It's coming!"

Elisha was the first to react. She hurried forwards, grabbed the door handle and pulled the door to the corridor shut. Then she turned and pushed her mum and Jay away from the door, further into the large hallway. "Come on! We have to get out of here!"

For a moment, Jay stood there in the hallway, staring at Elisha, struggling with the realisation that they had left his dad behind. They had *abandoned* him. But what else could they do? Whatever was in that room was coming for them now. It would be just moments before it reached the door and opened it.

"Upstairs!" Elisha hissed. "We have to get upstairs."

"But we have to go back for Dad." Mrs Slade stared at the closed door in front of her. "We have to—"

"It's coming to get you!" the sinister voice echoed around the hallway.

"No, we have to get out of here!" Elisha told her,

pulling her towards the main staircase leading up to the first floor. "Come on!"

Obediently, Mrs Slade headed up the stairs, flanked by her children. The sound of their footsteps was dampened by the threadbare red carpet. It only took a few seconds to reach the top, where they found themselves on a U-shaped landing with a tiled floor the colour of dried blood. Like the floor below, most of the tiles were cracked and chipped. Dust settled over everything like a decaying skin. In front of them, the pink neon sign glowed bright and cheerful.

DR KILGORE'S HOUSE OF HORRORS

They stopped and scanned the landing. There were doors on either side, but were any of them open? There was no way of knowing, but before they could even think about where to go next, the neon sign flicked off at the same time as the chandelier above the main hallway.

If it weren't for the light from Jay's phone torch,

still glowing in his hand, the building would have been in total darkness.

Jay held his breath and listened.

"You hear that?" Elisha whispered.

Shhh. Shhh. Shhh.

The faint sound of shuffling came from the room downstairs. Feet dragging on the dirt that covered the path in the display room.

Then came a gentle metallic rattling. The sound of a door handle turning.

It was followed by the creak of hinges, and Jay knew – he *knew* – it was the door to the corridor they had just escaped from downstairs.

Then the shuffling sound was in the hallway.

Slowly, deliberately, Jay directed his phone torch towards the sound, but it wasn't powerful enough to penetrate that far into the darkness.

"M-Mike?" Mrs Slade called out.

Shhhh. Shhhh. Shhhh.

"It's not him," Elisha whispered. "It's not Dad."

"Oh God." The words escaped Jay's lips without him even knowing he was going to speak.

"What is it?" Elisha's voice was a strangled panic. "What is it? We have to get out of here!"

But Jay couldn't move. His legs were heavy and cold. His chest was constricted with fear, and his hand was gripping his phone so tight it was digging into his palm.

"Come *on*!" Elisha snatched the phone from Jay's hand and pointed the torch across the landing. "This way!"

The physical contact snapped Jay out of his trance. He shook himself and followed Elisha and their mum across the hallway towards the first door on the right. He tried to ignore the hideous shuffling that was crossing the hallway below, tried not to imagine all kinds of terrors slouching towards him, eager to do unspeakable things.

When they reached the door, torchlight flickered over the plaque beside it that read: "TORTURE DUNGEON".

Then the light flashed downwards as Elisha reached for the door handle. When she fumbled to grip it, the phone dropped from her hand and tumbled through the bannister. It fell, flickering, to the floor below, where it landed with a crack and the light died instantly.

"The torch!" Jay uttered.

"Leave it!" Elisha told him. "Door's open! Come on!" The room was in darkness, but she headed inside, and Mrs Slade followed behind her. Jay hesitated.

Did they really want to head deeper into the House of Horrors? What terrors were waiting for them in the darkness of the torture dungeon?

But as he had those thoughts, the shuffling footsteps in the hallway reached the bottom of the stairs and began to climb.

"Hurry!" Elisha hissed at him. "He's coming!"

Jay had no choice. He took a deep breath and stepped inside.

As soon as they were all in the room, Elisha shut the door, and the three of them put their backs against it. They stood shoulder to shoulder, breathing the stale air and wondering what was climbing the staircase and shuffling across the landing on the other side of the door. Jay kept thinking about the way Sam had leapt from the waxwork set, axe tight in his large hand. The way his eyes had flashed behind the holes cut in the sack that covered his head. The way he had grinned like a hungry wolf.

Heavy breathing filled the air around them, a laboured, wheezing sound that rattled like dying breaths. Jay thought it was Elisha, but it couldn't be. Why would she be making a sound like that, breath rasping in her chest? It must be coming from somewhere else. Perhaps from the speakers that seemed to have been wired in around the house.

Wherever it was coming from, it was horrible.

And together with the shuffling that was moving closer and closer outside, it was enough to make Jay feel as if his whole world was fear. As if there was no point in even *trying* to survive or escape. It would be easier for him to just give up right now.

The shuffling stopped outside the door.

Whatever was out there, whether it was Sam with his axe and hood, or something else, there was just a few centimetres of wood between them.

"Oh God," Elisha mumbled.

Something pushed against the door.

Instinctively, Jay planted his feet firmly and pushed back. On either side of him, his mum and Elisha did the same.

Whatever was out there shoved harder.

Jay lurched under the force of it, but he held firm.

"Be strong," his mum said. "Be strong."

Jay could hear the waver in her voice and knew she was just as scared as he was – that she was being brave for his sake.

The door was shoved inwards again.

"Don't let it in," Elisha pleaded as if she were about to cry. "Please don't let it in."

Then suddenly: *BANG! BANG! BANG!*

Something pounded hard on the door, hammering again and again and again.

The wood rattled and shook against Jay's back as fear flooded his veins.

And then, just as suddenly, the banging stopped. The heavy breathing stopped. And there was silence.

Jay had no idea how long they waited with their backs pressed against the door.

"Has it gone?" Elisha finally whispered. And Jay was about to tell Mum to get out her phone torch when spotlights in the ceiling lit up, shining into the far corner of the room to illuminate yet another display.

This one was designed to look like part of a

medieval dungeon. The walls were painted as dirty grey stones, with chains and handcuffs hanging from rusty bolts. Torture tools such as thumbscrews, long-handled pliers and ugly contraptions were suspended from hooks.

The centrepiece of this display was something that Jay recognised as soon as he saw it. He didn't need to read the sign beside it to know it was an iron maiden. There had been one just like it in a special museum exhibition he'd visited on a school trip last year. It was an upright, human-sized cabinet with a door that bristled with sharp spikes on the inside. When a prisoner was put inside and the door was closed, the prisoner would be pierced by the spikes.

The iron maiden Jay was looking at right now was open, with a waxwork man inside it. There was a black hood over his head, and he was so thin, his ribs were visible. His skin was tight over his bones. His body was punctured in multiple places, as if the iron maiden had recently been closed on him and then re-opened. Dark red blood ran from the wounds.

More spotlights clicked on, one by one, revealing other waxwork figures around the room, all of them enduring terrible torture. Signs beside each scene gave names to the horrors being inflicted: The Scavenger's Daughter; The Garotte; The Brazen Bull.

The nearest scene was of a thin, bare-chested man being stretched on a rack. Lying on the wooden bed, his hands were tied with rope to a winder at the top. His feet were attached with rope to a winder at the bottom. A hooded waxwork torturer was frozen in the act of winding the ropes to stretch the man, whose head was tipped back, his mouth open in a scream of pain. An angry scar ran the length of his chest, from throat to belly button.

And then the speakers began pouring the screams and wails of the victims into the torture dungeon. The sound of screams layering over screams, echoing through the room, was almost unbearable.

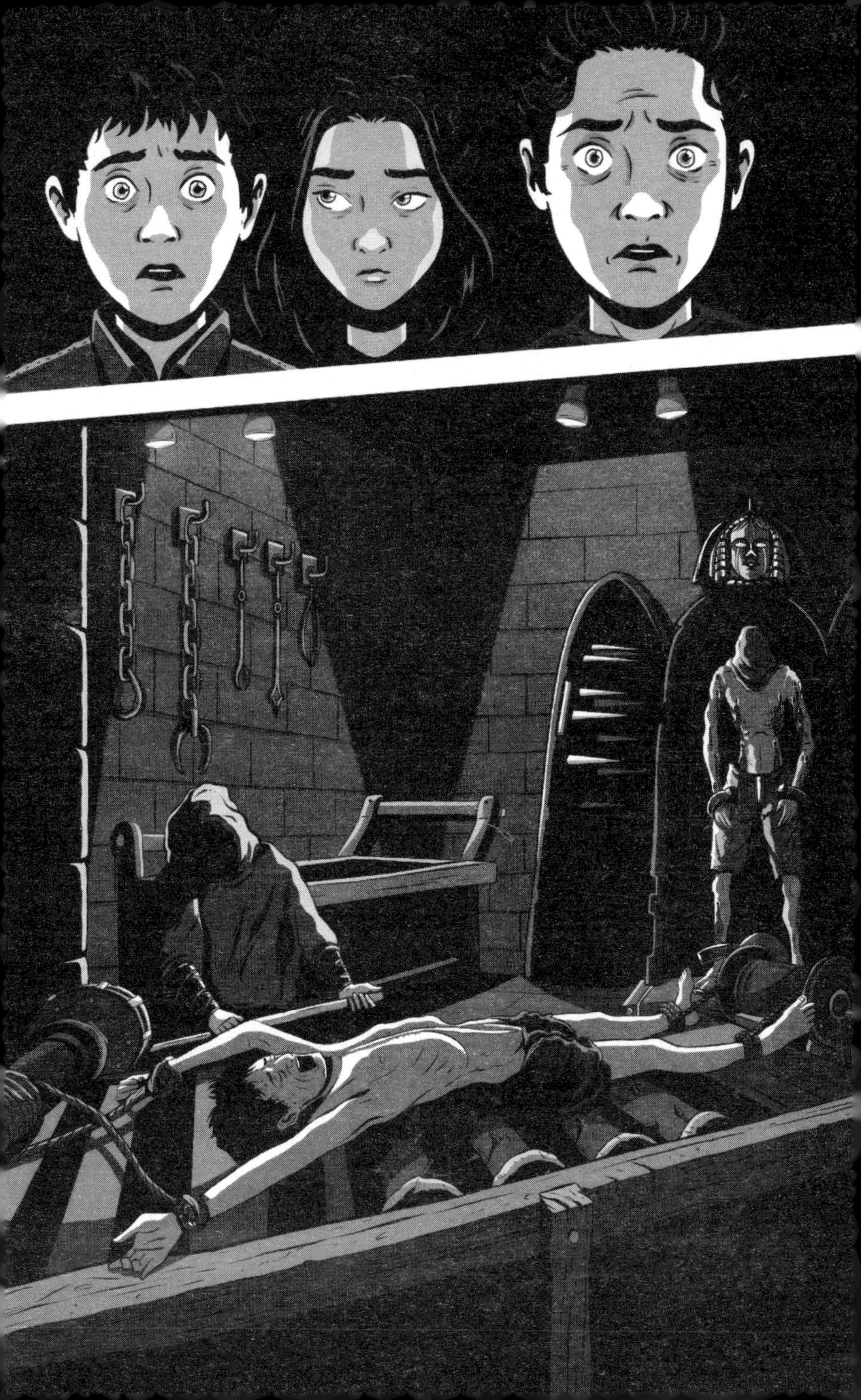

REPORT: X5J02032-1

Excerpt from: Messages between Stephen Hutson and Gary Benowitz of the FBI

Date: 27th July 2019 (four days after the incident at Coyote Creek)

Secretly obtained by Night House agents from phone records belonging to Gary Benowitz

---

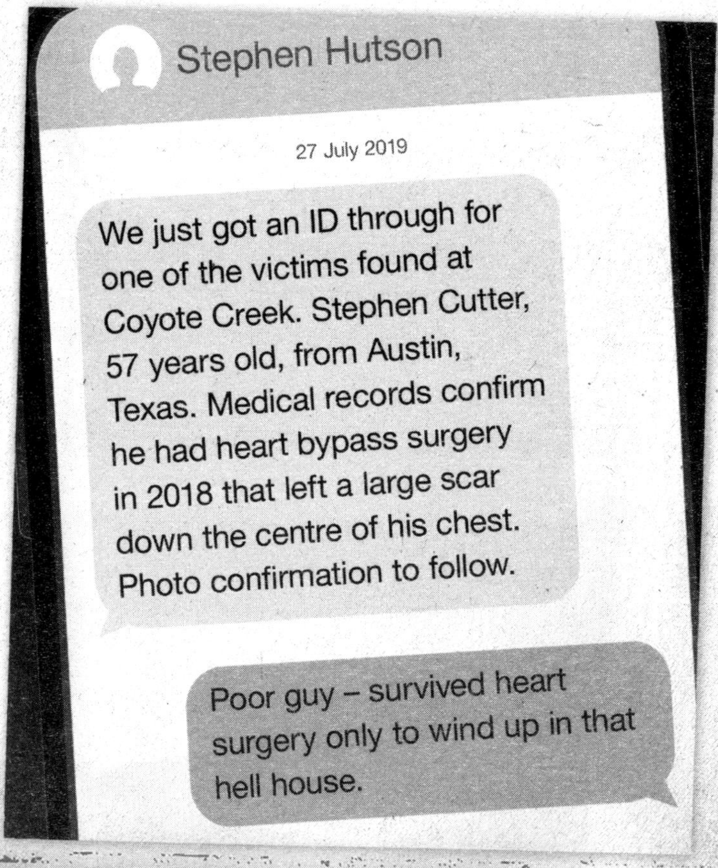

REPORT: X5J02011-4

CLASSIFIED

TOP SECRET

Interview with Jay Slade

Date: Wednesday, 31st August 2022

After the tragedy that happened to his family at Coyote Creek in 2019, Jay Slade was brought back to England, where he was placed in the custody of Dr Hooper at the Katja Psychiatric Institute. He was non-verbal for six weeks. When he finally spoke and told his version of events, Jay was diagnosed with "severe delusional disorder". He remained in the secure psychiatric hospital until August 2022 when, aged eighteen, Jay was released into the custody of his grandparents.

A Night House agent was able to speak with Jay in August 2022 by pretending to be a journalist investigating the incident at Coyote Creek.

JAY SLADE: It was bright in there, all the spotlights coming on at once. And some of those waxworks looked so real. Like, the scar on that man's chest ... it was just so *real*. And the whole time, there was all this noise coming from the speakers. Shouting and screaming and ... wailing. It was horrible. And I was watching the waxworks in case any of them got up and came for us, like in the other room.

NIGHT HOUSE AGENT: What was your mum doing at this point? And Elisha?

JAY SLADE: Mum was right beside me, holding on to me, trying to protect me, I suppose. But Elisha was freaking out. She was making everything worse by then. I mean, at first when we went into the house, she was pretty calm, but now she was winding us all up, getting hysterical. She kept saying stuff like, "Did that one move?", "Is it alive?" and "We have to get out." She was making me feel more scared. It was all on purpose though.

NIGHT HOUSE AGENT: We'll talk about that in a moment. First, can you tell me what happened next? I need to hear everything just the way it happened.

JAY SLADE: OK. So, I dunno, I suppose the next thing was that Mum saw the door at the other side of the room. It was painted the same as the walls – like it was a stone dungeon – but you could just about tell it was a door. Mum said she and I should stay against the door we'd come through, to stop anything coming after us, and Elisha should go to the other door. Make sure it was locked or block it to stop anything getting in that way.

NIGHT HOUSE AGENT: And is that what Elisha did?

JAY SLADE: No. She just freaked out even more, winding us up, going on about how we shouldn't block the other door in case we were blocking ourselves inside the room with something bad.

NIGHT HOUSE AGENT: Did you try to calm her?

JAY SLADE: Of course I flipping did! But she wasn't listening ... she was getting hysterical and saying all this horrible stuff about what might happen to us and where was Dad and ... I only realised later it was all on purpose. She was acting. She *wanted* us to be scared because—

(At this point, Jay's grandfather, Peter Slade, returned home and interrupted the interview. He was angry and concerned for his grandson. He made it clear that he would not allow the interview to continue. Jay became very agitated, reminding his grandfather that he was eighteen years old and legally an adult, but Peter Slade demanded that the agent leave the house otherwise he would call the police. The interview was terminated.)

Coyote Creek, West Texas Desert
Tuesday, 23rd July 2019

Jay couldn't stand Elisha's hysteria any longer. She was winding herself, and them, into an uncontrollable panic.

"He's going to get us," she said, breathless. "He's going to kill us all."

"Check the door over there," Mrs Slade tried to tell her. "We need to know if it's locked or not."

"I can't," Elisha babbled. "What if he's there? What if—"

"I'll go," Jay interrupted her.

He didn't want to leave his mum and venture

further into the room, but they had to do *something*. They couldn't just stand where they were and hope someone would come to rescue them. Jay had already run away once and left his dad; he couldn't do the same thing to his mum. And Elisha wasn't being much help.

"No, Jay," his mum argued. "Elisha should—"

"I'll go, Mum," Jay insisted. "It's fine. You and Elisha hold this door. I'll go and check the other one." Anyway, if he was honest with himself, he would be relieved to be away from Elisha for a moment.

"All right. Be careful," Mrs Slade said as Jay carefully took his weight from the door and stepped away.

Jay didn't know exactly what he would do when he reached the door at the opposite end of the torture chamber. He would have to think about that when he got there. The first thing was to get there and check whether it was open or locked.

He edged past the man being stretched on the

rack and crept across the musty room, careful not to make a sound. He weaved among the torture devices and grotesque waxworks. They were so lifelike and awful that he tried not to look at them, but his gaze kept straying to the iron maiden, which had been the first scene to light up. Something about it appalled him more than the other displays. And to make things worse, it was right beside the door he was aiming for.

As Jay drew closer, he had a real sense of how imposing the iron maiden was. The device must have been taller than Mr Emanuel – Jay's PE teacher and the tallest man he had ever seen – and was shaped like an iron sarcophagus. Except, up close, Jay could tell it wasn't really made of iron. Everything about it, every bolt and rivet, had been painted to look like metal, but Jay knew that if he went closer and knocked on it with his knuckles, it would *thunk* like heavy wood.

The thin, waxy-skinned man inside the iron maiden was wearing nothing but a pair of ragged grey trousers, cut off at the knees. His head was covered by a dirty black hood and had dropped forwards so his chin rested on his chest. A lattice of dark, sunken veins showed through the almost translucent skin that clung tight around his bones. Ribs and clavicles and shoulder joints were all painfully visible. And he was riddled with perforations where the spikes from the iron maiden had pierced his body. But now that Jay was closer, he could see other marks too. Smaller puncture marks on the man's arms and neck. And—

Jay stopped dead and stared.

Did the man just move?

He could swear that he just saw him move. The figure's chest had twitched as if he had taken a breath. Hadn't he?

No, Jay must have imagined it. Surely he was wrong?

He stared. And stared.

And waited.

And waited.

And then it happened again. It was only the slightest movement, but the figure's chest hitched up and down.

Jay took a step back.

Then the man's head began to lift. It rose up, slowly, slowly, until it was facing forwards.

Jay took another step back, imagining the face beneath the black hood. It would have bulging eyes and an open mouth. Broken teeth and a bloated tongue. Fear exploded inside Jay once more, as if it might overwhelm him and send him beyond the limits of sanity.

"No ..." Jay muttered.

The man's head turned slowly in Jay's direction, and, worst of all, he began to make a soft choking sound as he tried to form a single word.

It was a wet, desperate word that would haunt Jay's dreams for the rest of his life.

"Help."

Jay backed away from the hideous thing in the

iron maiden, desperate to get back to his mum and sister by the door. But even then, he would still be trapped. They couldn't return the way they had come for fear of whatever was lurking in the hallway. They couldn't go ahead because of the thing in the iron maiden. They were trapped, and there was nothing they could do. Things couldn't be any worse.

As if to prove Jay wrong, the lights went out once again, leaving him in the middle of the room in utter, utter darkness. Just a few steps away from him, that thing would still be there, in the iron maiden. Except maybe he wasn't. Maybe he was climbing out right now, clawing his way out and shambling towards him, arms outstretched, dry lips peeled back in a horrifying grin.

But the next sound Jay heard was from behind him. A strange rush of movement followed by a sudden gasp. A moment later, the lights popped back on, and Jay spun around to see his sister, Elisha, standing alone by the door.

Jay turned, scanning the room. The figure was

still in the iron maiden, head down, chin resting on his chest once more, but Jay's mum was gone.

"He took Mum," Elisha said, the tone of her voice rising. "He's playing with us. Why is he doing this?" Then she screamed out to anyone listening, "Leave us alone! Why are you doing this?!"

Without waiting for an answer, Elisha hurried across the room and grabbed Jay's arm.

"We have to get out of here," she said, dragging Jay towards the door beside the iron maiden. "We have to run!"

Jay had too many thoughts rushing around his head to object. He wasn't thinking straight. He was worrying about his mum and his dad. He was worrying about what was going to happen to him. He was worrying about the thing in the iron maiden and about what might be waiting behind the door Elisha was pulling him towards. He had too many thoughts in his head to notice the unnatural strength in his sister's grip.

Elisha yanked open the door to reveal a spiral staircase leading down.

"This way!" Elisha said, keeping a hand firmly gripped around Jay's forearm and leading him down the dimly lit stone steps. "Come on."

Jay wanted to object, but something was stopping him. He couldn't quite make his thoughts clear. It felt as if there was a fog over his mind, clouding everything. All he could do was follow. Obey. As if he had no choice.

At the bottom of the steps, Elisha pushed through another door and dragged Jay into the final nightmare. This was the truth of Dr Kilgore's House of Horrors. Nothing in his fifteen years of life could have prepared him for what he saw in that room. Nothing could have prepared him for the nightmare he was about to face.

Coyote Creek, West Texas Desert

Tuesday, 23rd July 2019

When Elisha dragged Jay through that final door, he faced one last scene of horror. A banqueting hall from hell.

He found himself in a large room with wooden flooring that was scuffed and marked and covered with dirt. Dust floated in the air, twinkling in the dull orange light thrown from a filthy chandelier that hung from a damp ceiling spotted with patches of black mould. The chandelier itself was made of bones that twisted and swayed in a gentle draft.

Several waxworks were placed around the edge

of the room, backs to the wall like palace guards. Except they weren't dressed in finery; they were ragged and skeletal, with features contorted into expressions of fear. They stood facing the large, ornate wooden table that occupied the centre of the room. There were seats for at least fourteen people at the table, but there were no place settings. Instead, the table was scattered with bones and feathers and scraps of fur.

Two people were seated opposite each other at the table. Their hands were tied to the arms of their chairs, and their heads were covered with black hoods. They were not waxworks – Jay could see that straight away.

They were his parents.

Behind each of them stood a tall, thin figure with its head lowered. These figures glistened in the strange light cast from the bone chandelier as if they were wet. Jay was reminded of one of the posters on the wall in the biology class at school – a poster of the human anatomy, showing how muscles and sinews and blood vessels interconnected. Like the poster, these figures wore no clothes and had no skin on their bodies or faces. Their veins and muscles and ligaments were clearly visible, twisting and coiling and connecting. Just a hint of white bone showed through in places. Jay wanted to believe they were unfinished waxworks.

Please let them be unfinished waxworks …

But he could tell that they were very much alive because the muscles in their chests expanded and contracted with each breath in and out, the sinews stretching and loosening.

A few moments after Elisha and Jay barged into the room, Jay's parents turned their hooded heads towards the sound and began making muffled noises as if they were trying to speak. They struggled against their restraints, rocking the chairs they were tied to.

At the same time, the two skinless creatures

turned to look right at Jay with yellow eyes that glowed from dark, lidless eye sockets. Black elongated pupils flashed in the centre of each eye. If they'd had lips, they might have grinned, but instead Jay saw only sharp teeth protruding from black gums.

Simultaneously, the creatures reached out with long bony fingers and gripped the hoods hiding Jay's parents' faces. In unison, they lifted the hoods so that Jay could look into his parents' eyes and see their terror.

It was a terror that flooded Jay's entire being. He felt as if he was finally losing his mind. This couldn't be happening. It wasn't real. It was impossible. His mouth opened, but he couldn't speak because his throat was constricted with fear. His eyes were wide, and his heart was racing so fast it was a hum in his tight chest. His whole body burned and tingled with adrenaline. It was all too much for him. Reality was slipping away.

Jay felt a firm grip on his arm, and he turned to stare into his sister Elisha's eyes.

Elisha grinned at him.

"Wh … Wha …?" Jay stammered. He tried to back away, but Elisha held tight.

"You think you're scared now, *bro*?" Elisha said. "Well, I know something that's going to *reaaaally* blow your mind."

"Wh …?"

Elisha clicked her fingers, and the full horror of Jay's nightmare hit him like a tidal wave. It rushed over him, smothering him, as realisation finally flooded in.

In that instant, Jay saw Elisha for what she really was.

And she was not his sister.

REPORT: X5J02012-1

CLASSIFIED

TOP SECRET

Interview with: Jay Slade

Date: Thursday, 1st September 2022

Although Jay's grandfather discontinued the interview on 31st August 2022, Jay himself contacted the Night House agent posing as a journalist the following day. Calmly and clearly, he explained that he believed the doctors at the Katja Institute had been "gaslighting" him and making him believe he was deluded. Talking to the "journalist" had made things clear for him, and he wanted to finish telling his story.

The Night House agent met Jay Slade in a busy coffee shop.

JAY SLADE: Thank you for meeting me. I don't think I have long, but I want you to hear what I have to say. Because you believe me. Don't you? I can tell you do.

NIGHT HOUSE AGENT: Yes, Jay. I *do* believe you.

JAY SLADE: Good. Because they didn't.

(The Night House agent notes that, throughout this interview, Jay spoke quickly as if he was in a hurry. He constantly scanned the coffee shop as if he was expecting someone or something.)

JAY SLADE: The doctors at the institute didn't believe me. Or, at least, that's what they said, but they haven't seen what I've seen. But you've seen things, haven't you? It's in your eyes.

NIGHT HOUSE AGENT: Tell me what happened in the dining room, Jay. You and your sister entered the room and saw your parents at the table with—

JAY SLADE: With those freaks standing behind them, yeah. Except it wasn't me and my sister, was it? It was me and one of those *things*. She clicked her fingers, and it was like someone took a hood off *my* head. Like the windscreen was dirty, and when the wipers went across, I suddenly saw things as they really were. I didn't have a sister, see? I never did. I'm an only child.

NIGHT HOUSE AGENT: I'm confused. So who was Elisha? Was she—

JAY SLADE: Don't you get it? *She was one of those things*. Those freaks. She must've got into the car when the tyres burst. Or maybe she flagged us down before that. I keep having dreams of her standing at the roadside, with her skinless face, waving to make us stop. I dunno, my memory's all twisted, but when she got into the car, she must have hypnotised us or something.

NIGHT HOUSE AGENT: So, to be clear, you're saying that Elisha was one of those creatures – like the ones in the dining room? And she hypnotised you into thinking she was your sister?

JAY SLADE: Exactly. Like the voice said in the House of Horrors about Skinwalkers. They can control your mind. So Elisha controlled our minds.

NIGHT HOUSE AGENT: You think she was a Skinwalker?

JAY SLADE: No. I don't think so. I think she was something else. They were ...

(Jay became quiet for a few seconds, as if he was struggling to say something.)

NIGHT HOUSE AGENT: What is it, Jay? What do you think they were?

JAY SLADE: I can't even make myself say it. It sounds ridiculous.

NIGHT HOUSE AGENT: It's just a word, Jay.

JAY SLADE: No. It's … Do you have a pen?

NIGHT HOUSE AGENT: I'm sorry?

JAY SLADE: A pen. Do you have a pen?

NIGHT HOUSE AGENT: I do.

(The Night House agent notes that they gave Jay a ballpoint pen, and Jay took a napkin from beside him on the table. He wrote on the napkin and passed it across to the agent. There was a single word in the centre of the napkin, written in capital letters.)

JAY SLADE: See what I mean? It's ridiculous. But it's true. I saw it. I *saw*. There are things out there people wouldn't believe.

NIGHT HOUSE AGENT: And it's our job to help them believe.

JAY SLADE: Right. Exactly. And she was controlling us. Elisha was controlling us like we were hypnotised. And now I think about it, it's so obvious. Everything we did was because of *her*. *She* told us to trust Sam. Why else would we have let him take us to that place? We only went into the house because *Elisha* told us it would be safe. Even inside the house, everything we did was because *she* told us to. She was in control the whole time.

NIGHT HOUSE AGENT: Why do you think that was? Why did she want to control you?

JAY SLADE: To make us go to the house. Because they wanted to … they wanted to … feed on us. Like they must've fed on all those other people and turned them into those horrible waxworks things that weren't waxworks. They weren't *waxworks*; they were people who'd been sucked almost dry but left alive. Maybe it was for if those things wanted a snack or something. But we were fresh, weren't we? We were *full*.

NIGHT HOUSE AGENT: So why didn't they just feed on you, Jay? If they could control your minds like that, why not just feed straight away? Why go to all the bother of bringing you to the house and leading you through the waxworks? Was it just for their amusement?

JAY SLADE: No. Don't you understand? It was to make us taste better.

Article taken from scienz4kids.com

scienz4kids.com

SCIENZ 4 KIDS

FEAR IS NOT JUST IN YOUR MIND!

You hear a whisper in the night and wake up to see a shape in a dark corner of the room. You feel your skin tingle and your heart beat faster. We've all been there. We all know what fear is. We know that when we're afraid, our heart races, our breathing quickens and our thoughts become muddled. Our skin feels clammy and tightens into goosebumps that makes our hairs prickle.

Oh yes, we all know what it's like to be scared, but did you know that there are lots of things going on *inside* our bodies when we are afraid? Did you know that fear floods our bodies with chemicals, preparing us for the "fight or flight" response?

As soon as humans recognise fear, the amygdala, a small part of our brain, sends messages to our nervous system. These trigger a very physical response. Our pituitary gland, at the base of our brain, releases a hormone called ACTH. This tells our adrenal gland to release cortisol, sometimes called the "stress hormone". The adrenal gland also releases adrenaline and a cocktail of other hormones into our bloodstream. All this causes a rise in blood pressure and blood sugar, giving us a burst of energy, preparing us for violent action. Or sometimes it makes our body freeze in an attempt to assess the threat and find a way to protect itself.

Coyote Creek, West Texas Desert
Tuesday, 23rd July 2019

Jay pulled his arm free and backed away from Elisha – if that thing was even called Elisha. He was trying to make sense of what was happening, but it was almost too unreal. It was as if a part of his mind had been missing for several hours and had now just come back to him.

The girl in front of him, who had been his "sister" for the past few hours, was not the tall, dark-haired girl with brown eyes he had been seeing. Instead, she was like the creatures that were standing over his mum and dad. Bald and skinless.

She was shorter, obviously younger than the other two, and she was wearing dirty trousers, a stained blue top, a leather jacket and filthy trainers.

Her clothes were too big and hung from her skinny frame. Her face was a network of muscles and veins, and the eyes that Jay had thought were brown were actually a bright yellow-amber, the black pupils oval and elongated. Her lipless mouth was filled with needle-like teeth.

Jay couldn't understand what was happening, but he knew that *this* was the real Elisha. Not the girl he had thought was his sister, but this *thing*.

"Jay," Elisha purred. "It's so good to have you here. I would love for you to meet my parents."

Elisha gave a little bow and swept her hand out to gesture at the two creatures standing over his parents.

"May I introduce you to Mom and Dad," Elisha said, her voice slipping into an American accent. "Dr and Mrs Kilgore."

The creatures gave their own little bows in return.

"And I, of course, am their daughter, Elisha Kilgore," she said. "It's so lovely to meet for real." She held out a hand as if she was expecting Jay to shake it, but all he could do was look down at it in horror.

Elisha's bony, skinless hand glistened wetly in the weak light. Her pearlescent fingernails grew to a curved point.

Jay struggled to pin down his thoughts. He was trying to work out what was happening. It was too bizarre. Too terrifying.

"Sam?" Elisha said.

Jay moved his focus from Elisha to a shadow that moved at the far side of the room. One of the waxworks stepped forwards to reveal himself as Sam, the man who had brought Jay and his parents to the house.

He didn't look like Elisha and the other two creatures. He looked human – exactly as he had looked when Jay first saw him. He was still wearing the jeans and plaid shirt he had been wearing earlier. He was also still holding the wicked-looking axe and wearing the cap he had stolen from Jay when he'd first entered the house.

Sam came to Elisha's side and looked down at Jay.

"Sam? Now we have made the introductions, won't you help Jay to the table, please? He's just *dying* for us to have him for dinner. It has been exhausting keeping him controlled for all this time." She looked into Jay's eyes. "You have a strong mind, Jay – you have been quite a challenge."

When Sam came forwards to take hold of him, Jay suddenly found his feet and shuffled backwards.

Sam took a step towards him.

Jay took another step back.

"Ah, do you feel it?" Elisha said. "Do you feel it rushing through you? All that adrenaline flowing through your blood? All those hormones?"

Sam stepped forwards again.

Jay took a strong step back.

"It's pumping around your body right now," Elisha said. "It has been spiking all night, preparing you for fight or flight. Making your stomach churn and your skin tingle." Elisha closed her eyes and made a strange sucking sound. "Delicious," she said.

Sam reached out to grab Jay, but Jay slipped to one side to avoid his grip.

"Oh, it tastes magnificent!" Elisha said. "Frightened blood is the most delicious. The most healing!"

As she said it, two things happened at once.

The first was that, from the corner of his eye, Jay saw the two horrors at the table lean down and sink their teeth into the back of his parents' necks.

The second was that Sam lunged at Jay and grabbed him by the front of his T-shirt. He held Jay tight and twisted him around so he was directly facing the two creatures feeding on his parents. He saw the way their throats moved as they drank, and he watched in horror as skin began to form over their bodies. It was as if they were making themselves whole by feeding on humans.

But Jay did not want to see it. And he did not want it to happen to him.

Jay lifted his foot and stamped his heel down as hard as he could on Sam's toes. At the same time, he thrust his elbow back into the man's stomach. Sam made an *oof!* sound as the air went out of him, and his grip relaxed. The axe that had been in his right hand clattered to the ground.

In that moment, Jay twisted and dropped, sliding out of Sam's grip. He picked up the axe and turned around, swinging it wildly. Sam stumbled backwards to avoid the blade, and Elisha dodged away, hissing at him, but Jay knew he wouldn't be able to overpower them. His only option was to escape.

When Sam came at him again, Jay slipped past him and escaped back through the door.

Coyote Creek, West Texas Desert
Tuesday, 23rd July 2019

Jay raced back up the spiral staircase and into the torture dungeon. As soon as he was through the door, he pushed it shut. He went to the iron maiden close by and put his shoulder against it. It was heavy and solid, but he shoved as hard as he could, rocking the iron maiden once, twice, then a third time. Finally, it toppled over and crashed down, blocking the door. Moments later, something strong thudded against the door on the other side.

"You can't escape!" Elisha hissed at him. "You can't run!"

The door began to push inwards, the heavy iron maiden sliding across the floor.

Jay frantically scanned the room. Thoughts of stopping to fight flashed through his mind – he had the axe, after all. But then the iron maiden slid forwards again, and the door opened enough for Elisha to peer through. Her peeled face glistened, and her yellow eyes flashed with excitement.

"You smell delicious," she crooned. "And I'm *starving*!"

All thoughts of fighting evaporated. Jay had to run. He had to escape.

Still holding the axe, he sprinted across the room and burst through the door into the hallway. Panic had hold of him as he raced across the landing, past the DR KILGORE'S HOUSE OF HORRORS sign, which was lit once again, buzzing gently and flickering pink light. He had no idea if the door on the other side of the landing would be open, or what was beyond it, but he went to it anyway.

It was unlocked.

Jay turned the handle, slipped inside and quietly closed the door.

—

It was dark and windowless inside the room, with just a sliver of pink light creeping under the door. Jay's eyes took a second to adjust before he could make out that he was in a large room that had black-painted walls and was packed with old furniture. Tables, chairs, cupboards, lamps and other unidentifiable objects were piled on top of one another as if this was a room for storing old junk.

It could be a good place to hide.

Jay heard Elisha emerge onto the landing.

"Where have you gone?" she giggled. "Which way now? Ooh, this is so much *fun*, Jay! I'm working up *such* an appetite!"

Jay dropped to his hands and knees, and crawled under the table in front of him. He made his way forwards, shuffling beneath some chairs, climbing over others, then turning to edge through a gap between a cupboard and a large wooden box.

Like that, Jay picked his way through the piles of furniture and junk until he was at the back of the room, far from the pink glow of the neon sign. Then he crawled under an old desk and paused in the darkness, like a rat hiding from a cat, and let his breathing settle.

Please don't let her find me. Please don't let her find me.

It was quiet.

No sound from outside. Just a gentle ringing in his ears and the *thud, thud, thud* of blood pumping through his veins.

Jay swallowed.

Please don't let her find me. Please don't let—

Tap.

What was that?

Click.

Oh no.

The door creaked open gently, letting more of the eerie pink light filter in.

"Jaa-aay," Elisha called in a lilting sing-song voice from the grave. "Jaa-aay, I know you're in here."

The door opened wider, spilling more light that slithered like a serpent beneath the piles of furniture, reaching out towards the place where Jay was hiding.

"I know you're in here, Jay. I can hear the blood pumping in your veins." Elisha's voice was as cold as ice. "It's like music. And I can smell you too. Sooooo delicious!"

Then came the sound of something – Elisha – clambering over the furniture. She stumbled and slipped, dislodging the piles, causing them to creak and tumble as she came.

"I'm coming for you," Elisha called, breathing heavily with effort and excitement.

That was when Jay knew he no longer had any choice.

Fight or flight. That was the human body's

response to fear, and he had tried flight. He had *tried* to run away. But there was no longer anywhere for him to go. His only option now was to fight. He had to be brave.

He took a deep breath, gritted his teeth and came out from beneath the desk where he was hiding. His muscles raged with adrenaline as he climbed up on top of the desk, gripping the axe tight in both hands. This was it. His last stand. He would fight to the end.

From his elevated position, Jay could see the shadow of a figure clambering across the piles of furniture. Elisha came towards him like a twisted, feral animal, eyes shining in the dark.

"Aaaah," she sang. "*There* you are."

A chill ran right through Jay, and he stepped back against the wall, raising the axe, ready to swing. As he lifted it above his shoulder, the back of the axe head knocked against the wall, making a gentle hollow sound.

The windows.

The thought popped into his head as if from nowhere. What had his mum said?

Where are the windows? Why can't we see any windows?

She had been looking at the front door to the building, and Jay now understood her confusion. When they had arrived at the house, they had seen windows on either side of the front door. But from the inside, there didn't appear to be any windows. The answer was so simple – they must be boarded up. It made sense. The windows were all boarded up and painted black to blend in with the walls. And that must have been the hollow sound the axe made just now – Jay was standing against the place where a window was covered over.

And if there was a window, there was a way out.

Without wasting a second, Jay turned, raised the axe and brought it down on the wall with as much force as he could muster.

There was a loud, splintering *CRACK!* as the axe slammed into the flimsy black-painted board covering the window. The blade went through and stuck tight, so Jay wrestled it out, twisting the axe from side to side. When it came free, the wood split further, and a crack of daylight appeared.

Jay vaguely wondered how long he had been in the House of Horrors, but he couldn't waste any time. He had to keep going.

"No!" Elisha shouted, and her movements became more frantic as she scrambled across the piles of furniture.

Jay swung the axe again.

This time the sharp metal head went right through the split, and when Jay yanked it back out, it ripped away a large chunk of wood. More daylight streamed into the room.

"No-no-NOOO!" Elisha screamed at him.

Jay swung the axe again, tearing away more of the board.

Behind him, Elisha screamed in pain, and there was a clatter as if she had lost her footing on the mountain of furniture and slipped down among the chairs.

Jay ignored her. He continued to smash the board, swinging the axe again and again.

Elisha continued to scream.

After one last good hit, Jay put a hand into the gap, gripped the edge of the wood and pulled. Splinters pierced his skin as he yanked the board away from the window. It tore off with a loud rip, and he threw the board aside as light streamed into the room.

"Nooooo!" Elisha screamed with a horrific gurgling howl as if she were drowning.

Jay didn't pause. He used the axe to smash the glass and clear it away from the windowsill. He was almost free.

He went to the edge and looked down. It was a long drop, but if he landed carefully, he should be all right.

As he was about to jump, Jay finally dared to turn and look into the room for the last time.

What he saw made his stomach turn.

There was a trail of oozing gunk leading from the edge of the desk he had been standing on, across the furniture to a wonky cupboard at the far end of the room. There, squeezed into a small corner of shadow on top of the cupboard, a shape lay twisted and moaning.

Jay realised that it was Elisha ... or what was left of her.

REPORT: X5J02012-2

CLASSIFIED

TOP SECRET

Interview with: Jay Slade

Date: Thursday, 1st September 2022

Although Jay's grandfather discontinued the interview on 31st August 2022, Jay himself contacted the Night House agent posing as a journalist the following day. Calmly and clearly, he explained that he believed the doctors at the Katja Institute had been "gaslighting" him and making him believe he was deluded. Talking to the "journalist" had made things clear for him, and he wanted to finish telling his story.

The Night House agent met Jay Slade in a busy coffee shop.

NIGHT HOUSE AGENT: Was Elisha dead?

JAY SLADE: I don't know. I didn't stay long enough to find out. But I don't think so. I mean, do ... *whatever she was* ... actually die?

NIGHT HOUSE AGENT: I don't know, Jay. What do *you* think?

JAY SLADE: Sunlight stops them, right?

(The Night House agent notes that Jay still couldn't bring himself to say the word. Instead, he tapped the napkin in front of him with the single word written on it.)

JAY SLADE: Well, that's what kept her away from me anyway. So maybe I'm right. Maybe that *is* what she was? Or maybe there isn't a name for what she was. What do *you* think?

NIGHT HOUSE AGENT: I just need all the facts, Jay. And I'm thinking about Sam. The one who picked you up on the road that night. You saw him later, didn't you? In daylight?

JAY SLADE: He was different. Like, he was human. I mean, don't *they* have ... familiars? Humans who do stuff for them during the day?

NIGHT HOUSE AGENT: That's the legend.

JAY SLADE: Well, maybe it's not just a legend. Maybe it's true.

Coyote Creek, West Texas Desert

Tuesday, 23rd July 2019

Jay tried to break his fall by bending his knees and rolling, but his left ankle twisted awkwardly. It bent to one side with a sickening crunch that fired a stab of pain up his lower leg. He struggled to his feet and limped away from the house.

The desert sun was already bright and hot. It beat down on his head and shoulders like a weight, and the brightness of it hurt his eyes after having been smothered by the darkness inside the House of Horrors. His ankle was agony, and his hand was stinging where the splinters had pierced his fingers and palm.

Even worse was the thought of what he had left behind. His mum and dad were still somewhere inside, but there was no way Jay could go back for them. He knew he wouldn't stand a chance. His only option was to find help. He had to get to the road.

So he limped on, dragging his left foot as he made his way past their rental car, still on the back of Sam's truck, and away from the House of Horrors. He hurried along the dirt track until he found himself on a wider road that must have once been the main street of what was now a ghost town.

Patches of dirty black tarmac showed through the orange dirt that lay across the road. A collection of rickety buildings slouched on either side of it. The first one that Jay passed was an empty, roofless stone building with shattered windows. The glass was like jagged blades in termite-riddled wooden frames. Beside it was a swimming pool, but it had been a lifetime since it had heard the splash of clear water and the laughter of children. Now it was filled with twisted metal and tumbleweed lying in the dirt that had blown in over the years.

There were more buildings flanking the disappearing road. Some were built from crumbling stone, others had sun-bleached wooden walls and corrugated iron roofs that were rusted and full of holes. Some were too decayed and weather-beaten to even tell what they had once been.

Jay limped on, past buildings with collapsed roofs and broken walls. He was so focused on escape, he didn't notice the faded sign that said "Joe's Store" or the brown lizard that startled and scuttled away under the dilapidated porch.

Jay was panting hard. The pain in his ankle was growing worse, his hands hurt and the heat from the sun was becoming unbearable. His breath was coming in gasps, so he slowed down and continued along the road, passing under a sign which told him he was in "Coyote Creek".

When he heard the sound of an approaching

engine, Jay's first thought was that it might be someone coming to his rescue.

Jay turned and looked behind him to see a black van turning off from the track to the House of Horrors. It sprayed dirt from its tyres as it skidded onto the road and began heading towards him.

Dust billowed in its wake.

It was coming for him.

And it was coming fast.

Jay knew his ordeal was not over yet, and he began to run once more. Every step was torture. Pain fired through his ankle each time his foot touched the ground. But the terror of being caught was far worse than any pain, so he endured the agony of it. Snot bubbled from his nose and spittle ran from his mouth as he gritted his teeth and limp-ran.

But Jay couldn't outrun a van. Somewhere in his fear he knew he would stand a better chance if he went onto the rougher terrain – a place where the van could not go. So he veered off the road and ran under the canopy of what might have once been a small petrol station.

He didn't look back as he headed behind the building and scrambled up a rocky slope on his hands and knees. Grit cut through his jeans, tearing at his skin, but when he reached the top, he kept going, never stopping. He limped between scruffy tufts of grass and dragged himself through spiky cacti. He stumbled on the rocky ground, continuing until he could no longer hear the sound of the van's engine, and when he looked back, there was no sign of anyone following him. In fact, he had come so far that he could no longer even see Coyote Creek hidden in the shallow valley he had escaped from.

Jay turned in a circle, looking for any clue as to where he should go now, and then he spotted it. Not far ahead, mostly blocked from his view by the terrain, was a black strip snaking through the desert.

The highway.

Hope.

Limping along the highway, it was only a few minutes before Jay heard the sound of an engine. Afraid it might be the black van, he dropped to the ground. Lying in the dirt, hidden by the scrub, he listened and watched but couldn't tell where it was coming from.

He tilted his head and held his breath, trying to—

There.

A glint of something in the distance to his right. Jay squinted and waited, watching the sunlight flicker until he saw what it was. Sunlight reflecting from the windscreen of a large truck rattling along the highway in his direction. This was it. This was how he would escape.

Jay struggled to his feet and began limping towards the oncoming truck. But soon he heard a second engine. This one was close and approaching from the other direction.

Without stopping, he looked over his shoulder to see the black van moving at speed behind him and to the right. It bumped across uneven terrain, smashing through cacti, kicking a trail of dust behind it. Tyres screeched as it jostled down a ridge onto the highway and skid-turned to race towards Jay.

Sam was at the wheel, staring through the dirty windscreen, grinning, relentless in his chase. He was still wearing Jay's cap – the one his mum and dad had bought for him at the UFO museum in Roswell.

Jay began to run. If he was quick enough, and if the truck reached him in time, maybe he could escape.

But the van was coming quickly. Its growling engine getting louder and louder.

Jay limped and limped, hoping against hope.

The truck was still some way ahead of him when the van screeched to a halt right behind him and the door clattered open.

Jay glanced back to see Sam jump down from the driver's side and run after him.

The fear of it bit into Jay, giving him a new burst of speed. His ankle screamed in pain, but he gritted his teeth and ran. His heart hammered. His mouth was dry. His eyes bulged with fear and pain. He pushed himself as hard as he could, but he wasn't quick enough.

Sam's heavy footsteps gained on him, thumping on the road.

Thump. Thump. Thump.

Jay felt Sam's breath on the back of his neck, then strong hands grabbed his jacket and dragged him backwards. His feet slipped out from under him, and he fell back, slamming his head hard on the surface of the road.

He looked up and saw Sam leaning over him. Fury burned in his eyes.

REPORT: X5J02013-1

Emails obtained from account belonging to Peter Slade, Jay's grandfather

Worried about Jay

From: Peter Slade

Date: 31 August 2022 12:52

To: Dr Hooper, Katja Institute

Dear Dr Hooper,

I thought I'd better get in touch to let you know that I returned home today to find Jay talking to a journalist about that horrible business that happened to him in America. I didn't know he was meeting anyone, and I told them to leave the house immediately or I would contact the police. Jay was agitated for the rest of the afternoon, and I'm worried he might get ill again. I would appreciate any advice you can give me.

Yours sincerely,

Peter Slade

Re: Worried about Jay

From: Dr Hooper, Katja Institute

cc Bcc

Date: 31 August 2022 12:59

To: Mr Peter Slade

Dear Mr Slade,

Thank you for letting me know. It is imperative that Jay does not speak to anyone about his experiences. He has made good progress, but even the slightest upset could bring back his delusions. Please do not contact the police under any circumstances – it could cause Jay a lot of distress. Instead, here is my personal telephone number ([redacted]). Please text me immediately if there is any suggestion that Jay might speak to the journalist again. Please also keep me updated with regard to Jay's health. If there is any deterioration in his state of mind, we must act quickly.

Yours sincerely,

Dr Hooper

REPORT: X5J02014-1

Excerpt from: Messages between Peter Slade, Jay's grandfather, and Dr Hooper of the Katja Institute

Date: 1st September 2022

Secretly obtained by Night House agents from phone records belonging to Peter Slade

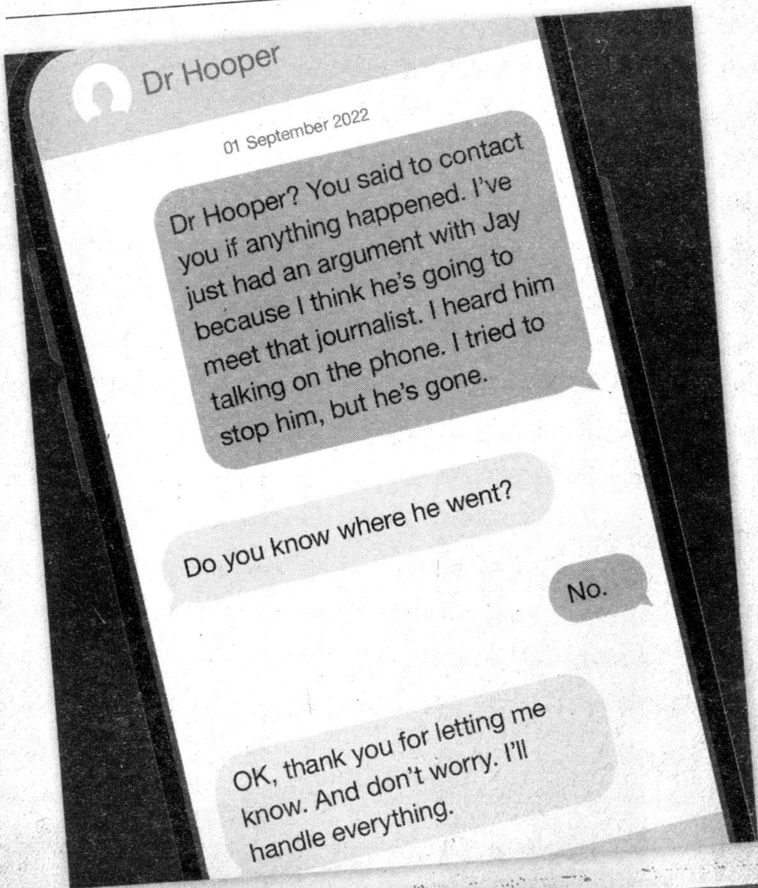

REPORT: X5J02012-3

CLASSIFIED

TOP SECRET

Interview with: Jay Slade

Date: Thursday, 1st September 2022

Although Jay's grandfather discontinued the interview on 31st August 2022, Jay himself contacted the Night House agent posing as a journalist the following day. Calmly and clearly, he explained that he believed the doctors at the Katja Institute had been "gaslighting" him and making him believe he was deluded. Talking to the "journalist" had made things clear for him, and he wanted to finish telling his story.

The Night House agent met Jay Slade in a busy coffee shop.

JAY SLADE: I thought that was it. When Sam got me, I thought I was a goner cos he pulled me up and grabbed hold of me. Like, he had his arms right around me, you know? I thought he was going to drag me into his van, and I'd be dead. But then I saw that truck still coming towards us. One of those big trucks they have in America. You know, those really big ones you see in films? I thought the driver must've seen us, and maybe I still had a chance. So I wriggled and kicked as much as I could, as *hard* as I could, flailing about and trying to make him let go. And it must've worked because somehow I was suddenly free and running straight for the truck. I don't think I even cared if it ran me over, but it didn't. It skidded to a stop, dust everywhere, and this woman climbed down and she had a gun, and when I got to her and turned around, Sam was getting back into his van. Then he just drove away.

NIGHT HOUSE AGENT: And it was over.

JAY SLADE: No. It isn't over.

NIGHT HOUSE AGENT: What do you mean by that?

JAY SLADE: I mean that it isn't over for me. I mean, I'm still here, aren't I? I still have nightmares. Still, no one believes me.

NIGHT HOUSE AGENT: I believe you.

JAY SLADE: Yeah... well.

NIGHT HOUSE AGENT: Do you know the trucker's name?

JAY SLADE: No one ever told me her name. She took me straight to the police, I think. I'm not really sure. It's all a bit blank after that, like I fell down a black hole or something. You know? Like I just shut down after everything that had happened. It's the "trauma" – that's what the doctors keep saying. So they brought me back to England and stuck me in that … "institute". A place for people who've lost their minds or something. But I haven't lost my mind. I'm not making this up like they say I am.

NIGHT HOUSE AGENT: So how do *they* explain what happened to you? If it didn't happen the way *you're* telling me, what do *they* say?

JAY SLADE: Well, these people came to talk to me—

NIGHT HOUSE AGENT: Police?

JAY SLADE: No, not police. Like police, but something else.

NIGHT HOUSE AGENT: National Crime Agency, maybe? FBI?

JAY SLADE: Maybe. Dr Hooper can probably tell you. Anyway, they told me my mum and dad were killed by some kind of deranged family. They said the family was killed when police went into the house, but ... I don't think so. Elisha is still out there. I can *feel* her.

(The Night House agent notes that Jay leaned forwards, staring into their eyes, and they saw that he was still afraid. Deep down, Jay was more afraid than anyone they had ever seen.)

JAY SLADE: She was in my head, you know. Right in here. She put thoughts in there, confused me, made me see things. The police or whoever they were can tell me I'm wrong, but I'm not. The doctors can tell me it's a delusion, but it's not. I know what I saw. I know what happened. And

I think there's still part of her in my head. Like a stain. I can *feel* her. And I know she's still out there, somewhere. *She's still out there.*

(The Night House agent notes that at this point the interview was interrupted when two men entered the coffee shop and approached the table. Jay did not struggle when the men escorted him from the premises. It was as if he knew there was no point in trying to resist. He told the agent they had "come from the hospital". The men put Jay in the back of a car and drove away. Night House agents learned later that Jay was returned to the Katja Institute, where he remains to this day.)

News article taken from the MIDLAND TRIBUNE, dated 24th July 2019

Yesterday afternoon, Mrs Emilia Flores, a trucker from Pasadena, California, prevented the attempted abduction of a young boy on the highway close to the former mining town of Coyote Creek. Information from the boy led police to a building in Coyote Creek that had been converted into a waxwork museum. There, police encountered a deranged family of serial killers that has been preying on passing drivers for several years. The family resisted arrest, shots were exchanged, and all members of the family were killed.

There was no further mention of the incident in this or any other news outlet.

NIGHT HOUSE FILE NUMBER FL1779:
The House of Horrors

Author's Conclusion

So there you have it. I have laid out all the facts from file number FL1779 for you to consider. And now it is up to you to decide if Jay Slade was telling the truth. Did he really spend the night in what he thinks was a vampires' lair? Did those creatures, whatever they were, really exist?

The authorities tried to convince Jay otherwise. They claim that he was wrong about what he had seen in the house at Coyote Creek. Their official version states that the Kilgores were a criminal family, that they resisted arrest, and that they were killed in an exchange of gunfire.

But Jay never accepted that version, not

even after spending months in the Katja Institute, which Night House agents have confirmed is a government-owned mental-health facility. In fact, it is the same facility to which Jay was taken after his final interview with an agent from the Night House on 1st September 2022. Jay remains in the institute to this day, and all attempts to speak to him have been blocked.

Except, those aren't quite *all* the facts. There is something I have held back because I wanted you to read both Jay's version of events and the FBI's version of events before I give you the final evidence from the file. This evidence was recovered by Night House agents, and I reveal it to you in the following pages. In my opinion, this damning evidence strongly backs up Jay's version of events.

This is the truth they didn't want you to hear.

REPORT: X5J0203

Excerpt from: Messages between Stephen Hutson and Gary Benowitz of the FBI

Date: 24th July 2019 (one day after the incident at Coyote Creek)

Secretly obtained by Night House agents from phone records belonging to Gary Benowitz

---

Stephen Hutson

24 July 2019

Can confirm we removed 32 victims from the house at Coyote Creek. Some fresher than others. All of them drained of blood, like the ones found in Atlanta in '97. Preserved and posed like last time. We have to stop these people – or whatever they are.

What about the Slade boy?

REPORT: X5J02035-1

Stephen Hutson

He's not talking. Poor kid. Can't even imagine what he's been through. We'll get him sent back to the UK. Tell him the same cover story we used in Atlanta. Same thing we gave the news channels. There's a facility in the UK where we can put him. The doctors will reinforce our story.

Good. Any sign of the parents?

No. We think the Kilgores took them. Fresh "snacks" for the road. I'll give you more details when we meet.

Uncover more truths . . .

The truth no one wanted you to hear
THE HOUSE OF HORRORS
THE NIGHT HOUSE FILES
"Absolutely horrifying!" JENNIFER KILLICK
Dan Smith
Illustrated by Luke Brookes
978-0-00-879090-5
The truth no one wanted you to hear
THE GHOSTS OF GREY TOWERS
THE NIGHT HOUSE FILES
Dan Smith
Illustrated by Luke Brookes
978-0-00-879091-2
Released: Oct 2026

THE NIGHT HOUSE FILES